Kirklees
METROPOLITAN · COUNCIL

Cult...
Red...
Hud...
KT-471-119

THIS BOOK SHOULD ...

# JIMMY ZEST IS BEST!

Jimmy Zest is just too clever for words. He can outsmart his friends and sometimes he can even outsmart his teacher.

But Jimmy Zest is at his best when he and his mischievous mates do some funny fishing, have a run-in with a white elephant and cry foul at a football match.

550 527 748

# JIMMY ZEST
# IS BEST!

## Sam McBratney

*Illustrated by Tim Archbold*

First published in 1985
by Hamish Hamilton Children's Books
This Large Print edition published by
BBC Audiobooks Ltd
by arrangement with
Macmillan Children's Books
2005

ISBN 1 4056 6078 3

Text copyright © Sam McBratney 1985
Ilustrations copyright
© Tim Archbold 2002

All rights reserved

**British Library Cataloguing in Publication Data**

Mc Bratney, Sam
  Jimmy Zest is best!.—Large print ed.
  1. Zest, Jimmy (Fictitious character)—Juvenile Fiction
  2. Inventors—Juvenile fiction  3. Children's stories, English
  4. Large type books
  I. Title  II. Archbold, Tim
  823. 9'14[J]

ISBN 1-4056-6078-3

Printed and bound in Great Britain by
Antony Rowe Ltd., Chippenham, Wiltshire

# Contents

| KIRKLEES CULTURE AND LEISURE SERVICES | |
|---|---|
| ACC NO. | 550 527 748 |
| CLASS NO | |
| Order No. | |
| Date | |
| Price | £9.95 |
| Supplier | |
| Loc | CPL |

# 1

## *Introducing Mr Olderfleet*

It was only the third day of the school term and some people were complaining already about their new teacher, Mr Olderfleet.

Legweak, for example, objected to his shoes.

'They squeak when he walks, you know,' he suddenly announced at breaktime. 'They sound like a couple of mice.'

'Good,' said Shorty, 'he can't sneak up on you.'

'Well I don't like his brute of a beard,' claimed Mandy Taylor. 'It makes his face look really, really itchy.'

'And did you hear him calling the roll?' cried Penny Brown. 'That's the third day in a row he's called me *Elizabeth* Brown and I don't like it. And I saw you laughing, Gowso!'

Gowso glanced up indignantly. At

that moment he was playing chess with Jimmy Zest and had just blundered away his Queen.

'I did not laugh, it was Shorty.'

'Nope,' said Shorty, patting his yellow yo-yo up and down, 'must have been Knuckles.'

Knuckles Alexander, Shorty's twin brother, sat beside Gowso, apparently fascinated by the battle at the chessboard. Secretly, though, his right hand fiddled with the buckles of Gowso's schoolbag so that he could pinch the flask out of it.

Pinching Gowso's flask was a favourite classroom game. Usually he brought hot chocolate, soup or tea.

'Stop your moaning,' Knuckles told Elizabeth Penelope Brown. 'It's your first name, isn't it? It's on your birth certificate.'

Penny glared at him. Of course this was exactly the kind of comment she expected from people like Knuckles Alexander. He couldn't possibly understand how she might be embarrassed, for he had a brain the size of a pea.

2

All the same, she wasn't the sort to let him get away with it.

'Look, Nicholas Alexander, I don't feel like an Elizabeth. I never have and I never will feel like an Elizabeth, so up your nose!'

'Checkmate!' declared Jimmy Zest.

Gowso sat back, defeated once more, and grabbed his schoolbag off Knuckles.

Shorty slowly crossed the room, patting his yellow yo-yo up and down, up and down.

'Why don't you tell Mr Oldfeet your name's not Elizabeth?'

'Because, Shorty,' explained Mandy Taylor, 'she's only known him for three days, that's why. We don't know what he's like behind that beard!'

Until the end of last term the wonderful Miss Quick had been their teacher, and they had known absolutely everything there was to know about Miss Quick. They knew the name of her pet canary, that her first name was Margaret, that she took her holidays in France and that she kept golf clubs in the boot of her red Mini. They all knew exactly how much talking they could get away with in class.

Now all that knowledge didn't matter any more, it was wasted.

Instead they had practically a total stranger for a teacher! A man with a black beard and funny shaped ears from playing rugby (so said Jimmy Zest), the first male teacher some of them had ever had. Mr Olderfleet. The name was so peculiar that Shorty couldn't say it properly and simply called him Mr Oldfeet.

Even Knuckles had been on his best behaviour and no one had raised more than a whisper.

Penny Brown turned to Jimmy Zest, who hadn't said much about their new teacher, apart from the theory about his flat ears.

'What do you think about him, Zesty—do you like him?'

The others listened carefully. Jimmy Zest was one of those people whose opinions could not be ignored.

'I think it's too early to tell,' said the cautious Jimmy Zest.

'He could be a monster. Mark my

words,' said Penny Brown.

Knuckles and Legweak, meanwhile, had discovered Gowso's flask hidden behind a curtain and were making the most of a rare and marvellous opportunity. They tossed the flask into the air and caught it just before it smashed on the floor.

'Over to me, here!' cried Shorty, frantically stuffing his yo-yo into his pocket just in time to pluck the spinning flask out of the air.

'Did you see that, Gowso!' Shorty shouted out in ecstasy. 'What a catch!'

The flask crossed the room in a series of arcs from Shorty to Penny Brown, to Mandy Taylor, then right over Gowso's head into the arms of Jimmy Zest. Curiously, Gowso didn't seem to mind that his liquid refreshment was flying about the place. Normally he put on such a scowl that his face deserved to be in horror pictures—which made the whole thing so much more entertaining. This time he sat at the chessboard grinning like a good sport.

Then Shorty grasped the flask after

the fashion of a Scotsman about to toss a very short caber, and almost hit the roof with it.

'Catch it, Legweak!'

The flask was in the air, falling awkwardly. Legweak, stretching, managed to get his hands to it, but the shiny  flask slipped away from him and landed on the floor with a squelchy, messy-sounding thud.

Flute! thought Penny Brown.

'That was a stupid throw, Shorty.'

'It was not indeed, Legweak, you've got hands like buttered toast.'

Jimmy Zest picked up the flask and shook it gently. They all heard the swilling mush of broken glass and tea, or soup, or possibly hot chocolate.

And now, thought Penny Brown, there'll be a big emotional scene. Nobody on the planet Earth could sulk like Gowso, they might not get a word out of him for a whole week after a thing like this.

But he didn't seem to care very much. He sat at the chessboard, quietly interested.

'What was in it, Gowso?' asked Mandy Taylor, not without sympathy. 'Soup?'

'Don't ask me, it's not my flask.'

Gowso opened his bag and proved it. His was snugly tucked away among his books.

'Well whose is it, then?' asked Shorty, puzzled.

As far as they knew, nobody else in the class brought a flask to school with the exception of Mavis Purvis, but her flask was a thing with a wide neck for stew, and anyway, if you looked at it twice she straight away told the teacher and got you into trouble.

Jimmy Zest screwed off the top and sniffed the escaping steam.

'Coffee.'

So who drank coffee? Nobody. The mystery, if anything, was cloudier still—until Jimmy Zest came out with one of his horribly logical opinions.

'I think that this flask must belong to Mr Olderfleet.'

An icy hush fell over the company. A distant bell struck the end of breaktime, and poor Legweak suddenly appeared to be heating up inside, for he now beamed redder than a lobster. WE'VE BUST HIS FLASK. The words might as well have been tattooed on his forehead.

Penny Brown said, 'Flute!' very quietly. Shorty pursed his lips to whistle, but no sound came out. He was thinking that Mr Oldfeet was not a small man—he probably had a voice that could blast you off your feet.

8

'Well, it wasn't me,' Gowso said in a loud and somewhat shaky voice. 'I'm going to tell him it wasn't me.'

And Mandy Taylor added, 'I told you! I said this was bound to happen to a flask one of these days, but you never listen to a single word I say, Shorty Alexander!'

'Who, me?' said Shorty, as if there were several other Shortys in the room. But he was worried. Already people were drifting back for the start of lessons. Since there was no time to decide what to do about the sudden crisis, the dud flask simply sat there on the window sill, in full view, for three-quarters of an hour. By means of hurried whispers and extravagant mime the entire class came to know about the disaster, and as time went by, the tension became unbearable. Legweak nibbled at his lips as if they were delicious and Shorty could not sit still. Mandy Taylor didn't dare look at the flask while Gowso, on the other hand, found it impossible to take his eyes off it.

Then Penny Brown started to

wonder what would happen if Mr Olderfleet decided to have a drink of his coffee at lunchtime! An ambulance would have to be called. Flute! She could just imagine it tearing through the school gates at ninety miles an hour with its sirens screaming and that blue light flashing.

She wrote a note and passed it to Shorty.

**RIGHT SHORTY, TELL HIM. WHAT IF HE TAKES A DRINK WITH HIS LUNCH AND GETS GLASS IN HIS STOMACH AND BLEEDING GUMS? YOU DIDN'T THINK OF THAT DID YOU?**

Shorty passed the note to Legweak, who had actually dropped the flask, after all. Legweak stuffed it into his pocket and chewed the end of his thumb.

About ten minutes of the school morning still remained when the scrape of a chair disturbed the quiet of the classroom.

Jimmy Zest was on his feet.

10

'Finished your decimals?' enquired Mr Olderfleet.

'Yes, sir. I did some extra.'

'Bring them here.'

Jimmy Zest did not move.

'Mr Olderfleet, sir, I must tell you that we had an accident at breaktime.'

'Oh?'

He said it quietly. Penny Brown thought she was going to pass out. They had only known him for three days, heaven knows what he was like! A real Frankenstein, maybe.

'We broke that flask—the one on the window sill. We thought it might be yours, sir.'

Maybe it's not, thought Penny. Maybe there was a secret flask-bringer in the class whom they hadn't discovered yet. Mr Olderfleet walked to the flask, shook it gently, and drips of brown liquid oozed from the bottom.

'You're right,' he said. 'It was mine.'

Gowso jumped to his feet. He couldn't help it, he was desperate.

'It wasn't me,' he yelled. 'They're always flinging my flask about

11

everywhere. I had nothing to do with it.'

'Sir, Mr Oldfeet,' Shorty said urgently, 'listen, I'm never going to touch another flask again—flasks and me is finished, that's a promise.' And to prove it, he licked the forefinger of his left hand and crossed his heart with two huge strokes drawn from his hip bones to his collar bones.

Bonk! The flask hit the rubbish bin.

'All right, exactly how many of you were involved in this . . . accident?'

Five hands went up. Gowso made sure his hands disappeared. He sat on them.

Then, slowly, Mandy Taylor put her hand in the air—Mandy, who *never* got into trouble, whose daddy was in the PTA, who had certainly been one of Miss Quick's favourites.

She was mortified.

'From now on,' said Mr Olderfleet, speaking softly, 'everyone in this class will go outside at breaktime, unless there is heavy rain. Jimmy Zest, Noel Alexander, Nicholas Alexander, Elizabeth Brown, Amanda Taylor and Stephen Armstrong—you six will write a punishment and have it on my desk first thing tomorrow morning.'

'At nine o'clock sharp, sir,' Shorty promised faithfully.

'What are we going to write about?' asked Knuckles.

'Good question,' said Mr Olderfleet.

'Decide for yourselves. One of you people suggest a suitable punishment that fits the crime.'

He appeared to be looking at Shorty, which was a waste of time. Shorty had no idea how to punish himself.

'Sir,' said Jimmy Zest, 'I think we should write a short essay on how a Thermos flask works. For example, we could explain how a flask is used to keep things cold as well as hot.'

Wise up, Zesty, thought Penny Brown, who hadn't a clue how a Thermos flask worked.

'Agreed,' said Mr Olderfleet as the lunch bell rang. 'Now off you go.'

\*　　　\*　　　\*

The school day was over.

Coming down the school hill, Jimmy Zest talked about flasks. He tried to explain how a flask had a layer of nothingness inside it called a vacuum, but nobody was listening to a word he said.

Penny Brown exclaimed, 'How many times did he smile that whole day? I'll

14

tell you. One time, that's how many. One miserable smile. Imagine going through a whole Wednesday without even smiling twice!'

'Maybe he's got sore ears,' said Shorty, helpfully.

'And forcing you to pick your own *punishment!*' cried Mandy Taylor breathlessly. She couldn't get over the sheer cruelty of it.

'I don't think he likes us,' said Legweak, who was usually an optimist.

It was a thoughtful group of people who waited on the pavement for the patrolman to put them across the road. All of a sudden things seemed very different. A great change had come over their lives now that Mr Olderfleet had taken over from Miss Quick.

# 2

## *Mervin the Vermin*

On Monday afternoon Jimmy Zest's mother opened her mouth and screamed.

It was quite a short scream, but incredibly loud. Naturally Jimmy Zest abandoned his book of chess puzzles and rushed out to see what was happening. His mother did not often make such noises—certainly not when she was out in the garden hanging up clothes.

He found her on the path, clutching a white sheet under her chin like a giant bib, and with a look of screwed-up horror on her face.

She looked like a witch.

'I saw a rat! Over there in the corner. A huge rat! Eeeee-*yugh*.'

Now that is very interesting, thought Jimmy Zest, who was always on the lookout for something to investigate seriously. Rats were quite common, of course, but even so, Jimmy Zest had not met with many in his life. As a matter of fact he'd only ever seen them in the headlights of the family car, scuttling busily across the road at night with their humpy backs and trailing their naked tails.

There was a great deal he didn't know about rats . . .

'COME AWAY FROM THERE AT ONCE!' shrilled his mother.

'But I just want to see where it lives.'

'Leave it alone, you will not go near the disgusting thing,' his mother said, dumping the linen basket into his arms. 'I am going into the house this very minute to phone the council. Rats in my back garden! *Eeugh.*'

And with a great shiver, she marched through the back door straight to the phone.

Jimmy Zest sat on the stairs and listened while she gave the council a piece of her mind.

'I don't know what sort of rat it is,' she told the man in the pest department, 'and I don't *care* if it's just a water rat, I want *rid* of that creature. It's as big as a cat. And they breed like rabbits!'

Satisfied at last, she set down the phone. The council had agreed to send out people to take care of the problem.

Jimmy Zest, meanwhile, had been thinking. He knew for a fact that some of his friends would be very keen to see that rat, especially Knuckles and Shorty, who kept guinea pigs. Even Penelope Brown might be interested if the rat was as big as his mother claimed.

Maybe it was a super-rat.

'How soon will the man from the council be here?'

'Not soon enough!' declared his mother.

I haven't got much time, thought Jimmy Zest.

\*     \*     \*

Penny Brown, Mandy Taylor, Knuckles and Shorty, Legweak, Gowso and Jimmy Zest came down the hill after school.

18

Some of those people were complaining again about the behaviour of their new teacher. Mr Olderfleet made more and more mistakes with every passing day. First of all he regularly failed to wish them all good morning the way Miss Quick used to do. It was as if he couldn't care less what sort of a day they had. Then there was his habit of beginning each day with mental arithmetic instead of the much more traditional spellings. And, worst of all, they sometimes missed half their morning break because he didn't hear the bell.

'At least he's got your name right,' Legweak said to Penny Brown.

'About time, Legweak! Why does he make us sit in alphabetical order? Miss Quick never made us sit in alphabetical order, it's so old-fashioned. And he had no business shouting at you, Shorty.'

Shorty happily kicked his schoolbag as he marched along. His schoolbag sounded hollow because there was nothing in it. Mr Olderfleet had shouted at him because he'd been fighting with Knuckles to be last in the line.

Then Mandy Taylor remembered the awful homework they had to write for next Friday.

'Homeworks are supposed to last for half an hour, isn't that right?'

'That is correct,' said Jimmy Zest.

'So how are we supposed to write a story about "My Most Unusual Friend" in only thirty minutes? I just think it's abysmal.'

'I think it's OK,' said Knuckles.

Huh, thought Penny Brown to herself. It was all very well for Nicholas Alexander to take that attitude, it was a known fact that when *he* wrote a story it had no beginning and no middle— only an end. He wrote for six lines and just stopped.

'I'm going to write about my rat,' Jimmy Zest said.

At the mention of the word 'rat' Shorty stopped punishing his schoolbag, and Penny Brown—who liked to be kept informed about everything—said in a accusing way, 'You never told us you had a pet rat, Zesty.'

'You never asked me, Penelope. And it's not a pet.'

'Where do you keep it, in a cage?'

'No, it lives in a hole in our back garden.'

'What?' said Gowso. 'You mean it's *real*?'

Jimmy Zest explained. His mother had seen it first and hadn't been through the back door since. Special rat-catchers from the council were coming to get it, but in the meantime the rat had pinched cheese from his father's trap without springing it. Really, said Jimmy Zest, it was a kind of super-rat.

'Zesty,' said Mandy Taylor with a wrinkle in her nose, 'a rat is nothing to be proud of, you know. People who have rats keep them a secret.'

'*You* haven't got one,' Gowso pointed out.

'I don't want one, Gowso! They come out of the sewers, for heaven's sake, who wants a rat!'

'Please, Zesty, call it Trash,' pleaded Penny Brown. 'Will you? Trash is such a perfect name for a rat.'

She was too late. The super-rat had already been christened.

'Its name's Mervin. Mervin the Vermin.'

'That's a rotten name,' said Penny Brown, 'it's not as good as Trash.'

'Get a rat of your own,' said Jimmy Zest, 'if you want to call it Trash.'

Ten minutes later, a stealthy group of people crept round the side of Jimmy Zest's house. Fortunately his mother had gone into town, so they were able to watch in peace.

Shorty, Penny and Legweak settled themselves behind the coalbunker while the others took up hiding positions behind two battered old dustbins. Mandy Taylor fidgeted because she did not want to sit on the dirty ground in her school clothes. Secretly she hoped that Mervin the Vermin would not put in an appearance—she did not like creatures which lived under the ground.

'This is stupid,' she pointed out. 'Look at us! Hiding behind bins just to see a rat. If it was a baby wallaby or a

Bengal tiger—but a *rat.*'

'Shh!' Knuckles hissed at her.

Mandy glared at him as if he was something of a rat himself, but she didn't actually say anything. Nicholas Alexander was a very unpredictable person, and he frightened her.

They saw the head first. It poked out from between stones in the far bank, and that rat had whiskers bigger than a bow tie.

After the whiskers came the fat, fuzzy body scuttling along the ground in nervous fits and starts. Gowso could not take his eyes off the tail, which squirmed like something with a life of its own.

'Flute!' whispered Penny Brown softly. As if he'd heard her, Mervin the Vermin disappeared into the stones.

Jimmy Zest stood up. The show was over.

'Boy, that's some rat,' Shorty said seriously. He sounded disappointed that Mervin wasn't his.

'OK, so you've got a rat, Zesty,' said Penny Brown. 'What are you going to do with it?'

'I'm going to catch it and write about it for homework.'

Mandy Taylor stopped dusting down her school skirt.

'*Catch* it? You're not serious, Zesty.'

'Bacon!' cried Shorty. Nobody quite knew why.

But of course Jimmy Zest was serious, thought Penny Brown. This was exactly the kind of thing he was famous for. His head was so packed full of daft schemes and plots that she wondered how he ever got to sleep at nights.

He would catch Mervin the Vermin, make a book of tickets, and probably charge people money to come and

24

see it.

*     *     *

On Wednesday morning, as Mr Olderfleet walked round the quiet classroom in his squeaky shoes inspecting jotters for signs of carelessness, he tripped over something at the foot of Jimmy Zest's desk—and there was a dreadful clatter.

Actually, most of the noise was caused by Mr Olderfleet himself, for he lost his balance and bashed into an empty desk at the back of the room, and of course everybody turned to stare while he tried to rub the pain out of his kneecap. Knuckles Alexander even had the nerve to smile.

Mr Olderfleet did not look pleased as he picked up the object which had tripped him. It was a wire basket with red handles, the sort of thing used in supermarkets. The top of the basket had been neatly closed over a by a cardboard lid, and at one end Jimmy Zest had cut a round hole in the fine, wire mesh. This hole was covered by a flap which had a long piece of string attached.

Hanging from the roof of this contraption was a piece of streaky bacon.

'All right,' said Mr Olderfleet, 'I give up. What is it for, you? Come on.'

Shorty piped up. He couldn't help it—for once he knew the right answer.

'Zesty's got a rat, Mr Oldfeet, he's going to write about it for homework. You call it Mervin. The cage is a trap you see, and the bacon's mine. I brought it.'

'You didn't bring all the bacon,' said a voice from the back of the room, 'half of it's mine.'

'Who sneaked it out of the packet?' shouted Shorty, with a murderous look at his brother.

'QUIET'

Mr Olderfleet silenced the Alexander twins and turned, limping, to Jimmy Zest.

'Do you know about rats, boys? They can get dangerous.'

'True,' agreed Jimmy Zest. 'They brought the bubonic plague to Europe

26

in the fourteenth century, though actually it was the fleas on the rats. Some people in foreign countries like to eat them, they taste like barbecued chicken. Their babies are born hairless and blind. There are black rats and brown rats and water rats. Voles.'

Mr Olderfleet peered at Jimmy Zest as if hypnotized by a talking encyclopedia.

'Sir,' said Legweak, 'Zesty's the class genius. You want to know something, just ask Zesty.'

'Stephen Armstrong, when I want your advice, I'll ask for it. Until then, speak when you're spoken to. On with your work, all of you—and Jimmy Zest, get that trap under your desk before it kills somebody.'

Poor Legweak went scarlet. Penny Brown saw Mandy looking round at her and she knew exactly what she was thinking about Mr Olderfleet.

'BEAST' her eyes said.

*        *        *

At lunchtime Jimmy Zest carried his

rat-trap into the playground to give it a trial run.

They needed a dummy rat, so Knuckles took Gowso's left shoe and threw it into the trap. Three metres away, Jimmy Zest pulled the string and the flap fell neatly over the hole.

'Get out of *that*!' Shorty shouted at Gowso's left shoe. 'It works. You're a genius, Zesty.'

Indeed, the trap appeared to work. While Gowso hopped about the playground on one leg, his shoe was a helpless prisoner under the streaky bacon.

Legweak declared that Mervin the Vermin was doomed.

By twenty-five to four that afternoon they were all in position for the main event in Jimmy Zest's back garden. The two dustbins, placed side by side, concealed Jimmy Zest himself. Shorty and Knuckles, the next most important people—since they had supplied the bacon—crouched on either side of him. Shorty had twigs in his hair to make himself look like a bush.

Behind, leaning on those three, was Penny Brown. The curly mop peering over the coalbunker belonged to Gowso. Legweak was stretched out on the cement, as flat as a crocodile, while Mandy Taylor sat on her schoolbag, pretending to be bored.

Things did not go well at first. Shorty crushed Penny Brown's finger under his knees, causing both pain and noise; Mandy Taylor hit her funny bone on the handle of the bin; and Gowso complained that he had pins and needles in his feet.

Such problems were forgotten when Mervin the Vermin stuck his whiskers out of the hole.

'Oooo!'

'He smells my bacon!'

'Shhh.'

'Gowso, get your loaf down.'

The rat inspected the trap with cautious, jerky movements, clearly full of suspicion to see streaky bacon hanging in such an unnatural place. Jimmy Zest, who did not blink, who scarcely seemed to breathe, tightened the string around his pulling finger. Mervin put his head into the trap and backed out again, which fetched a whisper of agony from Knuckles.

'We should have fried the bacon!'

Penny Brown swallowed and it sounded like thunder in her ears. The rat was in—apart from its creepy tail.

Jimmy Zest's hand twitched, the lid snapped shut and Shorty was up on his feet, triumphant.

'Got him, we got him, yabbadabbadoo!'

Working quickly now, Jimmy Zest fastened the lid and warned the others that the fleas on the rat could probably jump two metres. To counteract this very real danger he produced a long pole and passed it through the handles of the basket. Knuckles took one end of the pole on to his shoulder, Jimmy Zest took the other, and with the rat cage swinging between them, they headed down the road.

'Hey, where are we taking this thing, Zesty?' asked Knuckles.

'The park.'

Marching down the public road, Mandy Taylor kept her lips shut tight as if afraid that a flea would hop into her mouth. Every time Gowso looked at the rat it seemed to be staring right back at him and he didn't like it. But Penny Brown thought that Mervin's pink little eyes looked rather tearful.

The park wasn't far, so they soon

arrived at a suitably secluded place near the bandstand, where Legweak and Shorty carefully eased the cage to the ground.

Mervin stared out passively. Gowso said, 'That rat keeps looking at me, you know.'

'It fancies you, Gowso,' said Legweak.

'Right, Zesty!' declared Penny Brown, hands on hips. 'We're here. Now that we've got it, what are we going to do with it, that's what I'd like to know!'

As it happened, Jimmy Zest had quite a number of suggestions as to what they might do with the rat, but Mandy Taylor spoke first.

She said two words. 'Kill it.'

Six pairs of eyes immediately fastened on the last speaker. Some of them were quite shocked—they had not expected to hear such strong words from Mandy Taylor, who was a non-violent person.

'Well it's only a rat,' said Mandy. 'They're the enemies of the human race.'

'That is a very serious thing for you to say, Mandy,' Penny Brown observed sincerely. 'It's a very serious thing to take another creature's life.'

'You wouldn't say that if it bit you,' said Knuckles. 'Let's bury it.'

Legweak was horrified.

'*Alive*?'

'Why not? What did we capture it for, then?'

'Not to bury the poor thing alive,' shouted Penny Brown. 'What are we? Monsters? This is your fault as usual, Jimmy Zest.'

They decided to have a vote—for or against the rat. Apart from Shorty, who wanted to vote against the rat but on the same side as Penny Brown, they quickly made up their minds.

Jimmy Zest counted hands.

'Four-three in favour of the rat. Right, that settles it, we'll just have to take it to the council. They'll know what to do with it because vermin are their responsibility.'

'Where's the council?' wondered Shorty.

'Town hall. Let's go.'

Off they marched, seven people, pole and cage, towards the centre of town. They passed the library and the museum. Just before they came to the police station Gowso claimed that it was surely illegal to carry a rat in public, so they paused while Legweak searched the litter bins for a piece of material to throw over Mervin's cage.

Presently they arrived at the town hall. Gowso, who had the front pole by now, slowed down to a halt when he saw the flight of imposing steps rising to the front door.

It was a massive door, wonderfully carved. Two lifelike stone lions squatted on either side of it.

'What's keeping you, Gowso?' said Shorty. 'The lions won't eat you.'

'Wait a minute, wait a minute,' said Gowso.

'*I* am not going in there,' said Mandy Taylor.

She, too, knew something about the council. Important people held meetings in there—people who governed the town. What would they think when a rat arrived in out of the blue?

But this was not a time for faint hearts. Penny Brown spoke from three steps up.

'Be like that if you want, Mandy—Mervin is the council's responsibility and I'm going in. Who else is coming?'

The answer was—everybody else but Mandy. They'd never been into the town hall before and this was the best chance they were likely to get. Even the timid Gowso saw that they were actually doing the council a favour, rather like the very famous Pied Piper of Hamelin, donkey's years ago.

He led the way through.

The floor of the town hall was tiled yellow and brown. It looked like a huge chessboard, sparkling in the radiant light from a high, glass dome. A broad staircase spiralled towards the gold-painted ceiling. While Shorty paused to wonder at a painting of a man in a red cloak—and white tights—Jimmy Zest read signs. Upstairs were BIRTHS, DEATHS AND MARRIAGES, but there was no mention of PESTS.

'There!' cried Shorty, pointing at a

35

sign saying RATES.

'*Rates,* Shorty, rates,' said Penny Brown. 'Not *rats.* Your spelling's dire!'

After some dithering, Jimmy Zest led the party into an office labelled ENQUIRIES.

A tall man in a checked jacket watched while Knuckles and Shorty manoeuvred the pole through the office door. The man in the jacket was about to speak when Shorty beat him to it.

'Mister, we've brought you a pest to deal with, OK? You call it Mervin. Get it up on the counter, Knuckles.'

The job was done. Carefully, Knuckles eased the pole from the handles of the basket, and when Jimmy Zest removed the piece of material from the cage, the man in the jacket was looking at Mervin the Vermin.

He did not speak. His eyebrows rose and disappeared under his fringe. In fact he looked so shocked and surprised that Penny Brown thought he was going to faint.

'Mrs Chapman,' he said in a whisper, without taking his eyes off Mervin.

'MRS CHAPMAN!' he yelled.

The trouble was that Mervin didn't behave himself, he scampered round the cage, rattling the bars now that he could see the world once again.

'Mervin, be good!' Penny Brown scolded him.

Mrs Chapman arrived and clapped a hand dripping with jewellery to her heart.

'Oh, glory be,' she said simply.

In the background, computer keyboards began to stop clicking, one by one. A secretary who had come closer for a look began to scream and dance on the spot, for something unexpected had happened. Mervin the Vermin had not been idle during his journey from the park and, cleverly working under cover, he had successfully gnawed through the flap string, and now he was poised on the edge of the counter as if contemplating a leap to complete freedom.

'Flute!' said Penny Brown.

Pandemonium occurred. Office staff deserted their posts, the man in the jacket dashed to the far side of the office, and when Gowso saw Mervin looking straight at him—again!—he just bolted.

The lady called Mrs Chapman remained at the counter, shouting, 'How dare you bring that creature in here. You will be prosecuted!'

Neither Knuckles nor Shorty liked that word 'prosecuted'. They left the office simultaneously—sprinting. And now, outside in the open street, Mandy Taylor could hardly believe her eyes. The terrified Gowso emerged from the town hall, took the steps in three jumps and whizzed by without speaking.

'What happened?' she cried after him.

The Alexander twins came next, followed by Penny and Zesty.

'What is it? Did something go wrong?' Mandy yelled.

'Run, you stupid balloon!' Shorty advised over his shoulder.

They all bolted across the road into a newsagent's shop, where they gathered in a frantic little huddle, for it had become apparent that one of their number was missing.

'What is going on? Will you please tell me,' demanded Mandy Taylor.

Shorty sucked in air. 'Zesty's stupid trap fell apart and Mervin got out. The council's got Legweak and they're going bananas.'

'We should split up,' said Knuckles grimly, 'and go home separate ways.'

They decided to wait a moment or two to see what happened. Mandy bought a comic so that the shop owner couldn't complain while they used his window to spy on the town hall across the road.

But the doors did not open, and Legweak did not appear.

'He'll be brought up before the mayor,' Gowso said with certainty.

In view of the grave situation they left the shop in twos, in case the council had people out looking for them.

'Meet at my house in half an hour,' said a grim-faced Jimmy Zest.

'If we make it!' cried Shorty.

\*     \*     \*

In rather more than half an hour's time the same six people met in Jimmy Zest's garage to consider their next move in these dramatic circumstances.

Everybody had a say, except for Shorty, who played with his yellow yo-yo. Penny Brown blamed Jimmy Zest for the whole thing, whereas Knuckles blamed Legweak for getting caught and voted to do nothing at all.

'But what happens if he talks?' objected Gowso, who felt sure he'd seen this kind of thing on TV 'Once the council start asking questions,

Legweak'll crack.'

It was agreed, eventually, that they should go round to Legweak's house and say he was a prisoner in the town hall: otherwise his parents would wonder why he wasn't in for his tea. Mandy Taylor was elected to do the talking on account of her very good manners.

On the way, they lost Gowso. A van passed by with four words painted along the side of it— BOROUGH COUNCIL CLEANSING DEPARTMENT—and he took off down the street like a clockwork mouse.

Mrs Armstrong came to the door. Mandy cleared her throat.

'Mrs Armstrong, Stephen . . . Stephen is . . . well he's . . .'

'Missus,' said Shorty, 'the council's got Legweak.'

Clearly, Legweak's mother did not have the slightest idea what he was talking about, so Shorty tried again.

'You see, we took Zesty's Mervin to the town hall, but they didn't realize we were doing them a favour. Anyway,

Mervin got out and Legweak got caught, that's why he's not in for his tea.'

That was the moment that Legweak himself appeared under his mother's arm at the front door.

'Talk to your friends, Stephen,' she said, 'or something will burn.'

Legweak's friends gaped at him.

'What are you doing here, Legweak?' Penny Brown asked him rather fiercely.

'I live here,' said Legweak.

'Well you'd no business getting caught, we were worried sick about you.'

When at last they all calmed down enough to listen, Legweak explained that the clerk had nabbed him while he tried to escape with the pole.

'You could have just let go, Legweak.'

'Naw. Fingerprints you see.'

Then they had evacuated the office and asked him a few questions, such as, had he been told to bring a rat to the office by grown-ups as a kind of protest?

'Then they let me go,' said Legweak, and went in for his tea.

On the way home with Jimmy Zest, Penny Brown began to think about poor old Mervin. Maybe, she thought, maybe he was really a mummy rat and had hairless little blind babies at home in her nest.

Where was he now, she wondered?

'Zesty?'

'What?'

'When they catch Mervin, what'll they do with him?'

'Give his body to science,' said Jimmy Zest. 'That's if they ever catch him.'

# 3

## *Bubble Trouble*

Mandy Taylor should have known better.

If she had wanted her birthday celebrations to pass off with the minimum possible fuss, she should have kept the news that she was having a party a closely guarded secret.

But she did not. She talked about the party in advance, raised false hopes, and got people excited by the coming event. Indeed, she even handed out invitations in public no matter who happened to be watching, and generally encouraged the idea that if you weren't going to her party then you weren't a particularly important human being.

On Friday afternoon the boys heard her talking loudly to Penny Brown.

'It's going to be a help-yourself sort of thing with *pâté* and crackers. Mummy wants sandwiches but I told her, Mummy, sandwiches are so *boring*. Anyway, if we do have them they won't have any crusts and we are taking a *Schwarzwälderkirsch torte* out of the freezer, you know, one of those German cherry things, but we don't know whether to buy meringue nests or make our own. We can barbecue cocktail sausages in the garden if it's dry so cross your fingers. There you are . . .' a small pink envelope changed hands '. . . that's your invitation, Penny.'

Jimmy Zest hovered with a question.

'What about us? Are we invited?'

'Did you invite her to your party, Zesty?'

'I didn't have a party.'

'Well then,' said Penny Brown, shrugging as if there was no more to be said.

'I let her see my rat.'

'Big deal, Zesty!'

Shorty had been dazzled by Mandy Taylor's chat about food, but he soon recovered.

'What was that German thing you've got in your freezer?'

'*A Schwarzwälderkirsch torte.*'

'There's no such thing,' said Legweak.

'There is so, Legweak. It's a big, chocolate cherry cake with mountains of cream and it's gorgeous.'

A rather dreamy look came over Shorty's face as if he could see in his mind's eye a substantial wedge of that big German cake with the tongue-twister name. And cocktail sausages! Shorty loved to puncture those fat little sausages with a wooden stick and gobble them three at a time—more than three if you squashed them.

Apart from the food, there was another reason why the boys wanted invitations to that party. The Taylors had money, admittedly not as much as Cricklewood-Holmesy, the neighbourhood millionaire, but enough to afford a large house with a very private garden. According to Legweak, who had seen over their wall, it was like paradise in there. The Taylors had a swinging garden sofa, a putting green, four real barrels and an ornamental garden pond with some multicoloured pipe-smoking gnomes. Mandy herself frequently boasted about the Taylor goldfish—one was nineteen years old and longer than your foot.

Gowso gave an audible sigh. He loved barbecues, he loved cream, he loved exploring the gardens of other people.

'Nobody wants to go to your rotten party anyway,' he said moodily.

'Just as well, Gowso,' Mandy Taylor told him, 'for you'll not be there.'

\*　　　\*　　　\*

On Saturday afternoon Mandy Taylor got the shock of her life.

It happened while she was helping her mother to weed the borders near the front gate. The Alexander twins arrived on Legweak's bike.

Nicholas and Noel Alexander stood on the lowest bar of the wrought-iron gate and peered through like a pair of monkeys at the zoo.

'Mandy, aren't those boys friends of yours?' asked her mother. 'I think

47

they're smiling at you.'

Of course she knew them! They were the two worst pupils in the whole school and they were up to something crafty.

Mandy dug fiercely with her trowel and tried to ignore them.

'Missus,' called Shorty, 'could we come in and talk to Mandy for a minute? We're friends of hers, you see.'

'Certainly, boys.'

When Mrs Taylor opened the gate for them, Mandy saw that Knuckles had a brown parcel under his arm. In they came, bike and all, staring round them as if they had just beamed in from another planet.

'Where do you keep the goldfish, Missus?' asked Shorty. 'I suppose they're round the back?'

'Yes, boys, round the back.'

'We got a present here,' said Knuckles, addressing Mandy. 'For your birthday.'

He held out the parcel. Really, what Mandy Taylor wanted to do most of all was simply disappear, but her mother said, 'Well, what a lovely thought! That's awfully nice of you, boys, it really is. And such a surprise! I'm sure Mandy is delighted.'

Mummy, stop gushing, Mandy was thinking. Her mother didn't know them, she didn't understand about Nicholas Alexander—how only yesterday he'd told Legweak's little brother that the catseyes in the middle of the road were *real* cats' eyes taken from *real* cats.

'Open your present, Mandy, and say thank you.'

'Thank you.'

'Don't mention it,' said Shorty, happily patting his yo-yo up and down.

Since the brown paper wasn't even properly stuck down the parcel practically opened itself in Mandy's hands.

It was bubble bath. A green plastic bottle of bubble bath. The screw-on cap was shaped like a sailor's hat and when Mandy examined the bottle it looked more than half empty.

'I have to go now,' she said breathlessly. 'I have to make a call.'

Off she dashed, round the back of her house and into the hall where she grabbed the phone, tapped some numbers, and glared at the green bottle while she waited impatiently for the ringing to stop.

'Penny? They came to our house! KNUCKLES AND SHORTY, who do you think. Yes! Right through our actual gate. Well I can't believe it either, I was mortified and guess what they've *done*.'

A gasp came down the phone. '*Bubble* bath? Flute.'

'*Boys*' bubble bath. *And* it's half empty!'

Penny Brown knew exactly what to do.

'Well, give it back to them, Mandy. You don't have to accept a present you don't want, this is a free country.'

'Do you think I should? You know what he's like.'

She meant Knuckles, one of those really impossible people who couldn't take no for an answer. There was no telling what he might do.

'Of course you should. Give it straight back to them on Monday morning, first thing. And if you don't, Mandy—I will!'

*       *       *

During that weekend Jimmy Zest read in an old geography book how primitive tribesmen used the medium of dance to end periods of drought, and make it rain.

So he sat down and wrote a rain dance of his own. It took him twenty minutes. On Monday morning he taught the Jimmy Zest Rain Dance to Gowso and Legweak, and the three of them pranced about the cloakroom twirling in unison while they bawled out the following words:

'Waala Woola Wumba Way,
Make it rain on her birthday,
Open clouds and do not cease,
Bucket cats and dogs and GEESE;
On her birthday make it DRIZZLE,
So the sausages cannot SIZZLE.'

And so on. There were several verses to the Jimmy Zest Rain Dance, each intended to make the heavens open on the day of the famous party to which they had not been invited. Shorty badly wanted to join in the fun, but Knuckles stopped him.

'*We* don't want it to rain, stupid,' he pointed out. 'Aren't we going to Mandy's party?'

Gowso stopped prancing about. He refused to believe it.

'You're not going. You couldn't be.' Mandy Taylor would never invite Knuckles.

52

'Well, you just go and ask her,
Gowso,' Knuckles said confidently. 'We
brought her a present last Saturday.'

Inside the classroom, away from the
racket going on outside, Penny Brown
and Mandy Taylor were asking one
another spellings when all of a sudden
they were surrounded by Knuckles,
Shorty, Gowso, Zesty and Legweak.

Gowso spoke with great feeling.
'Knuckles says he's going to your party
with Shorty. Is it true?'

Mandy was too shocked by the idea
to answer immediately, so Penny
Brown did it for her.

'How can he go to a party when
nobody has invited him? Wise up,
Gowso.'

'Look,' said Knuckles, pointing one
finger. 'We brought her a present,
right? That means we're going.'

He said it as if he had a ticket to get
in! Mandy Taylor twiddled the ring on
her little finger in dismay—he didn't
understand the rules about parties. He
didn't see that buying a present was not
enough, you had to be on a list.

'A present?' Penny Brown almost

shouted. 'Some present! A bottle of bubble bath, and it was half empty. You took it off your bathroom shelf and stuck some paper round it!'

'We did not, we bought it out of our own money.'

'Why did you buy boys' bubble bath, then?' This quick question silenced Shorty, but not Knuckles.

'What difference does it make? It's only for your skin, skin's all the same.'

'Mandy, just give it back to them. They'd turn up at the teddy bears' picnic if they knew where it was.'

The reluctant Mandy Taylor lifted the green bottle by the sailor's cap and stood with it as if life had become too complicated all of a sudden. Eventually Penny Brown put it firmly into Shorty's hands.

'There. You had no business buying her a present, everybody knows only girls are invited.'

Total war would have erupted there and then had a lookout not hissed that Mr Olderfleet was on his way down the corridor. Knuckles stared straight into Mandy Taylor's eyes.

'When's your party?'

'Don't tell the snook, Mandy.'

'Two o'clock this Saturday.'

'Right, we'll be there.'

Away he went, satisfied, and jumped into his seat at the back of the room like a cowboy getting on a horse.

Mandy's face was flaming, and Penny Brown knew why. Her birthday party wasn't on Saturday, at all, it was on Friday, after school. She'd just told Nicholas Alexander the wrong day!

'Serves him right,' whispered Penny. 'At least we got rid of that awful green bottle.'

Mr Olderfleet arrived. As usual, he was not smiling.

\*  \*  \*

Immediately after lunch Mr Olderfleet produced his register and patiently called the roll for the second time that day—yet another departure from tradition they all noted. Once had always been enough for Miss Quick.

There were five people missing. At the last moment Jimmy Zest slipped through the classroom door, and he sounded breathless.

'I'm very sorry, Mr Olderfleet. I was detained.'

'Oh, detained, were you? That's a nice word—detained. And what detained you, I wonder?'

Something was wrong, Penny Brown sensed it at once. Jimmy Zest was never late, he obeyed all rules. And why were his shoes soaking wet? And where were Gowso and Legweak and Knuckles and Shorty?

As if to answer all these questions, the caretaker burst through the classroom door with a great big brush in his hands, and he looked like a man at the end of his tether.

'Excuse me, Mr Olderfleet,' he said. 'I've been in this school for ten years and I never interrupt classes . . .'

True, thought Penny Brown, he never did!

'. . . but I have to ask you to come and look at the activity area next door. It's a mess, that's what it is, muck 'n' mess. I'll swing for 'em one of these days. Swing for 'em!'

And the great brush trembled in his hands.

When Mr Olderfleet left the room, the rest of the class rose as one and rushed to the windows. Luckily the activity room was just outside, so they had a clear view of what was going on.

Meanwhile, in the activity area, Shorty was having problems at one of the sinks. He stood with his elbows well spread out, trying to hold down the foaming monster which was swelling up in the sink and oozing over the edges. He pulled out the plug, but it made no difference. Those suds had a will of their own, they kept on rising.

Gowso had the same problem at the other sink, only worse. The suds had taken him over. His hair seemed curlier than ever now that it was decorated with a host of glittering little bubbles. He rather resembled a new kind of creature struggling to emerge from a frothy chrysalis.

'I can't stop it!' cried Gowso, beginning to panic.

'Turn off the tap, stupid!' shouted Legweak, who was skating merrily across the wet floor. So Gowso turned the taps, but anticlockwise, which made things worse. Another eruption of bubbles occurred.

'They can't be stopped, *nobody can stop them!*' screamed Gowso. He lifted huge soapy blobs from the sink and stared at them in sheer horror. Somewhere in there, were his hands.

Knuckles was loving this.

'Keep them coming, Gowso,' he called out deliriously as he ran through the mass of delicately coloured bubbles, thousands of bubbles, some going up, some coming down, selecting only those of the largest size for annihilation between the palms of his hands.

Then he realized that a dim shape at the far end of the room was moving, and that it was Mr Olderfleet, and that he was doomed.

The others had seen him too. Legweak dropped the green bottle, which bounced, being empty. Mr Olderfleet stared at a wobbly big bubble until it burst of its own accord right in front of his nose.

'I will see you boys in my classroom,' he said, 'in five minutes, when you have dried off. Stephen Armstrong, bring that bottle with you.'

Then he left. A look of total misery appeared on Gowso's face. 'I told you! Didn't I tell you?' he snapped wildly at Legweak. 'I told you to stop pouring it in!'

You could have heard a bubble burst in the silence when those boys crept into the classroom a little later, and lined up like four drowned rats. Legweak stared at the floor, Gowso rolled his eyes helplessly because he didn't know where to look and Shorty tried to explain.

'Mr Oldfeet, we were just washing our hands. Zesty said it would be a good experiment.'

'What with?'

'Bubble bath. They just started taking us over, you should have seen it. We couldn't stop them, sir, they came at us from everywhere, it was like The Invasion of the Bubbles.'

'You threw them round me!' shouted Gowso, almost in tears.

Mr Olderfleet removed the green plastic bottle from Legweak's hands.

'Why did you bring this stuff into school?'

'It's not mine, sir, it's Mandy Taylor's.'

Flute, thought Penny Brown.

When Mandy stood up to be interrogated, the shame showed on her face. And although Penny's heart was thumping like a drum, she stood up, too.

'Excuse me, Mr Olderfleet, but that bubble bath isn't Mandy's any longer. Nicholas and Noel gave it to her as a present but, sir, she didn't accept it.'

'Sit down, please.'

Penny Brown sank into her seat, crushed.

'As it happens I do not have time,' said Mr Olderfleet, 'to sort out the rights and wrongs of all this nonsense. You four boys will now mop up the mess you made, and you'll stay in tomorrow at lunchtime to make up the time you've lost. Mandy Taylor, write out ten times "I must not bring bubble bath into school". And now get out your books, for we have work to do on the decimal point.'

\*　　　\*　　　\*

All the way down the school hill, Penny Brown and Mandy Taylor fumed. They did not even smile at Mr Jones the patrolman, who had once been their friend, because he was one of *them*, one of that collection of grown-ups who ran the school, who blamed the wrong people and would not let them tell the true facts.

Mandy Taylor had been at school for six years and she'd never been in trouble. Now she'd picked up two punishments within three weeks.

'The man is inhuman,' she stated categorically.

'I bet he used to teach in some jail,' said Penny Brown.

*        *        *

On Friday afternoon, when the sky began to fill over with some rather menacing clouds, it seemed as if the Jimmy Zest Rain Dance might actually work. Indeed, Mandy Taylor thought she felt some spots of rain on her upturned face; but she persuaded her mother to light the barbecue anyway.

Happily the clouds did not burst, and soon the wind blowing about the garden smelt good enough to eat— Penny Brown hoped that it blew all the way round the neighbourhood, wafting the delicious, smoky aroma of sizzling sausages and lamb chops straight up the noses of Jimmy Zest and his demented rain-dancers.

The party seemed to be a huge success. Each one of the privileged guests said she had a lovely time, even the girl who fell on the patio during one of the games and skinned her knee. And, of course, there was lots to eat, for Mandy's mother was a wonderful hostess. Apart from some blackened pieces of meat and some rubbery trifle, the guests finished everything, especially the big German cherry cake. Mandy said '*Schwarzwälderkirsch torte*' so many times that Penny accused her of showing off.

On the Saturday Penny came round to help with the messy business of tidying-up. After scrubbing the barbecue pans and grills with steel wool they went upstairs to have another look at the presents people had brought. While Mandy lay on the floor in front of a black-and-white 750 piece jigsaw, Penny arranged the birthday cards along the window sill.

She was just thinking how she liked the funny ones best, when she saw them.

And she nearly died.

'Oh flute, Mandy,' she croaked. 'Would you *look*!'

'What is it?'

'It's *them*. They're here for the party!'

They were at the gate. They wore identical dark-blue blazers with silver buttons and both their ties were yellow. The Alexander twins had arrived spick and span, and with their hair nicely combed and parted. From behind her curtains Mandy Taylor could only stare at the change which had come over them—as if they were a pair of neglected antiques which had somehow come up marvellously bright.

'We forgot about them,' hissed Penny, 'and look, they've got a parcel.'

Another present!

Mandy Taylor winced with psychological pain. How on earth, she wondered, how could there be people in this day and age who did not understand about birthday parties, who did not recognize the word No. Where had they been all their lives?

'Penny, what'll we do?'

'Quick—down the stairs and stop them before they get to your door!'

'But what'll we tell them?'

'We'll say your dad's in the police. Come on.'

It was already too late. Mandy had only reached the bend in her stairs when the door bell rang and the knocker boomed and her mother came out of the kitchen to find out who could possibly be ringing the bell and knocking the knocker at the same time.

'Missus—' Shorty's voice carried up the hall, 'is Mandy in?'

'We're here for the party.'

'And we got her another present.'

'Black Magic.'

65

Mrs Taylor stepped back for a better view of the boys in the smart blue blazers.

'The party? But . . . you must have made a mistake, boys, the party is . . . well, it's over, frankly. It happened yesterday.'

After another glance at the parcel, which was daintily tied up with red ribbon, she laid a hand on the banister and called out, 'Mandy, could you come down here for a minute, please.'

Mandy appeared. Nicholas Alexander pointed straight at her.

'She told me it was Saturday.'

'Did you deliberately tell these boys that your party was today?'

'Mummy, they weren't invited, they just invited *themselves*. Please ask Penny, she knows about them, too.'

Vigorously nodding support, Penny Brown slowly descended the stairs. In the meantime Shorty, who was not a quick thinker, realized the awful truth.

'You mean we got here on the wrong day?'

'Well you're not getting our present,' Knuckles said truculently. 'We're going to eat them ourselves.'

'Eat them,' said Penny Brown.

'And they were Black Magic.'

'EAT THEM!' shouted Penny Brown.

Mrs Taylor stood by like a rather helpless doorperson while this was happening in her front porch. One of the boys ripped open the parcel with his teeth. And then, abruptly, the crisis ended. The twins departed, depositing pieces of their gift-wrapping paper all over the front drive. A few seconds later, a box of Black Magic chocolates, held high in an obvious gesture of defiance, sailed along the top of the Taylors' roadside hedge.

'Now do you see, Mummy,' cried Mandy Taylor, 'that's what they're *really* like!'

Five minutes later Knuckles and Shorty arrived, munching, at the public seat outside Worthington's sweet shop, where Jimmy Zest was chatting to Gowso about the six-a-side football tournament. Legweak stopped doing wheelies on his bike so that he could stare suggestively at the box of chocolates.

'You weren't long,' said Gowso, who loved gossip. 'What about the party?'

'We didn't get in.'

'Why not?'

'It was yesterday,' said Shorty, dithering over a coffee cream or a chocolate truffle. In the end he ate both.

While the boys sat on the seat feeding on Mandy Taylor's birthday present, Knuckles described some of the horrible things he planned to do on Monday to Penny Brown and Mandy Taylor. Just listening to him made Gowso's hair stand on end.

Then Jimmy Zest said quietly, 'I know something else you could do. Something you haven't thought of.'

'Too late for a rain dance, Zesty,' observed Legweak.

'I'll put coal in their schoolbags,' said Knuckles dreamily. 'I'm going to clip my toenails and . . .'

'You still haven't heard my idea,' interrupted Jimmy Zest.

They listened. Gowso was horrified by what he heard, he said they would all get arrested for sure. The others, however, could hardly wait until the following morning . . .

\*       \*       \*

It was a typical, sleepy Sunday spring morning on Cypress Avenue where Mandy Taylor lived.

An electric milk float purred quietly down the road. A red-faced jogger, all alone, ran by in a grey tracksuit, panting his steaming breath into the slightly chill air. Nothing else stirred save a furtive, tabby cat. The clouds were high and the weather was fine, though a thin haze over the neighbourhood made the distance somewhat vague.

That haze suited Jimmy Zest and his friends very nicely as they crouched behind the Taylors' back hedge. They did not wish to be seen this particular morning.

Legweak, the skinniest, wriggled through the narrow gap with the natural ease of a worm. Next came Shorty and Knuckles, then the equipment. There was a moment of concern when Knuckles's three-metre fishing rod—already assembled—got into a tangle on the way through.

'Pull it!'

'*Don't* pull it, twit.'

'Shhh!'

'OK, it's free. Come on, Gowso.'

Gowso shook his head vigorously. Now, at the moment of truth, he decided that he'd better stay outside and keep guard. To be caught raiding Mandy Taylor's back garden was an experience he could do without.

The others were safely through the hedge by now, and breathlessly surveying the expanse of new and unconquered territory which lay before them.

The garden had three distinct areas: one for growing vegetables—very ordinary; a recreation area with putting green and swinging garden sofa; and a large, ornamental pond conveniently placed near the rear of the garden.

It was all very quiet.

'What do you think?' asked Legweak, shivering slightly. He felt like a trespasser.

Jimmy Zest, obviously the general in charge of this operation, crouched behind a bush until he was certain that they hadn't been seen. The very house seemed to be asleep with its curtains drawn like closed eyelids. He signalled the way forward with a twitch of the net he'd made from a bamboo cane, a wire coat-hanger and a pair of his mother's tights.

'Right, let's go. And no talking.'

Fortunately, a plantation of young conifer trees screened the pond from the lower part of the house. The pond had an oval-shaped rim of crazy paving, which supported the smiling gnomes. The leaves of a water lily floated on the surface, and below these, in the depths, there were occasional flashes of silver and reddish-gold.

'I see them, I see them!' whispered Legweak, so overcome with excitement he almost fell in.

But he'd brought nothing to fish with, he could only watch the action.

As Jimmy Zest lay on his belly, net at the ready, a worm on a hook dropped gently past his ear and plopped in the water. The Alexander rod was so long that the twins had to stand well back to land their float in the pond; and since neither twin would allow the other to use it on his own, they fished together, four-handed, from six metres away, as if they expected to catch a whale.

In this way, with many nervous glances at the house, they went after one of Mandy Taylor's goldfish.

Two minutes went by and nothing happened. Then, 'You got a bite!'

'Shhh!'

'But you did, the float squiggled.'

'Legweak, shut up, you'll get us caught.'

Knuckles decided that they were probably snared in some weed, but just as he reached for the float to shorten the line, the float bobbed.

And then it went under. Right under.

'Shorty! Your float, your float!'

Shorty staggered like something possessed, the rod jerked in his hands.

'Have I got one? Have I, have I? What?'

'Get it in, Shorty.'

'I got one? Have I? Is it weed?'

'Reel—will you *reel*.'

Shorty reeled, but he'd never actually caught a fish before and didn't really believe what was happening to him—and not until he saw the tumultuous thrashing in the water did he realize the awesome, exhilarating truth: an actual fish was doing battle with him.

His mouth opened and he yelled.

'I got one. I got a fish, a fish!'

'Ah, come on, Shorty,' said Jimmy Zest, anxiously scanning the house, 'why don't you just send them a postcard and tell them we're here.'

Knuckles sprinted to help his delirious brother. Legweak knocked a stone gnome into the water and had to scoop it out again—he therefore missed the heart-stopping moment when Mandy Taylor's goldfish, wriggling and gleaming, came clear of the water on the end of Shorty's line.

For a moment or two, all four of them were lost in admiration when they saw their prize lying tangled up in Jimmy Zest's mother's tights. The biggest goldfish they'd ever seen was not much larger than a big toe; this one was longer than your foot, and a rich, red-golden colour with grey and white blotches along the back.

'Goldfish freckles!' breathed Shorty.

Legweak felt quite sorry to see it lying there with its sides heaving. Quickly, Knuckles removed the hook and slid the fish into Zesty's bucket.

74

They did not intend to harm this marvellous creature—just kidnap it for a while.

'Right, let's go.'

'Ah, come on, Zesty, we can get another one,' said Shorty, whose blood was up.

'No! I said *one* fish. They could be up any minute.'

The adamantine Jimmy Zest led his raiding party to the back hedge, where they left by the same hole they had come through. They found Gowso at the far end of the street, where he had gone just to be on the safe side.

'You're all crazy. I heard you lot yelling your heads off,' he complained bitterly.

Shorty thrust the bucket under his nose. 'There you are, Gowso—meet Jaws.'

'Huh. Very funny!'

Shorty laughed so much he had to set the bucket down and lean on Legweak.

The successful party now proceeded along the main road in the direction of the old bridge over the disused railway, and while they walked Jimmy Zest explained that goldfish were actually carp.

'The Japanese developed them as ornamental fish. Or maybe it was the Chinese.'

Shorty stopped walking. 'You mean this here fish came all the way from China?'

'He means the original goldfish,' said Gowso.

'Oh, I see.' Shorty sounded relieved. He reached up and set the bucket on the parapet of the bridge, intending to take a rest. Knuckles turned round to say that he'd like to send the fish to Mandy Taylor through the post—and disaster struck. He nudged the bucket over the edge of the bridge with the tip of his rod.

Of course it was a complete accident, but that was no comfort at all to the five people who now peered over the bridge, every one aghast. Water and bucket and goldfish and all had disappeared on a very long drop.

'Well that's it, now it's done for,' declared Gowso in a shrill. 'There you are!'

Not quite yet! They were faced by a stiff climb over a barbed-wire fence, but there was no hesitation, for this was now a matter of life and death. Knuckles, first over, plunged headlong down a twisty little track with Legweak behind him, both disregarding brambles and nettles and wicked-looking gorse in a bid to a reach the stricken goldfish in the nick of time.

They found the bucket by the side of the old track. Shorty arrived, wide-eyed, sucking in lungfuls of air. This wasn't any old fish, he'd personally caught it.

'Have you got it? Yes?'

They showed him the bucket. It was empty.

'Over here,' called Jimmy Zest. He'd found the fish snared in the prickles of a gorse bush. The marvellous carp lay across both his palms, and it did not move.

Shorty stroked it in silence. He was upset. For nineteen years it had been swimming round Mandy Taylor's pond in small circles, and now . . .

Gowso came running up. 'Well? Is it dead?'

'Put it this way, Gowso,' said Legweak, 'its parachute didn't open.'

The boys fought their way back up the bank in single file, and on to the bridge again.

'She'll find out, you know,' Gowso said miserably, dismayed by a mental image of Mandy Taylor throwing a fit. 'She'll miss it, there'll be murder!'

'Don't be a looper, Gowso,' said Knuckles, 'it's a secret. How's she going to find out?'

'Maybe she counts them every night.'

'No way,' said Shorty. 'Did you see it going for my worm? The things weren't even half-fed.'

As Shorty walked down the road, the tail of the ornamental carp could be seen dangling from his left trouser pocket.

# 4

## Baked Beans and White Elephants

Mandy Taylor climbed up on a classroom chair in order to make an announcement.

'OK, everybody, listen, who belongs to this? I found a yellow yo-yo.'

'Mine!' yelled Shorty.

'So it *is* your yo-yo. Right, what were you doing in my back garden, Shorty? That's where I found it, and one of our gnomes is chipped on the head.'

'Give him a headache tablet,' said Shorty.

'So you don't deny it?'

'I do deny it,' said Shorty. 'I wasn't near your back garden.'

'Then this can't be your yo-yo.'

'It is my yo-yo.'

Penny Brown, who loved to be involved in all that was going on, couldn't help joining in.

'Shorty, if this is your yo-yo, you

must have been in her back garden and if you don't see that then you need glasses.'

'It flew off my finger and went over her hedge.'

Not for a fraction of a second did Mandy Taylor believe this feeble explanation, but Shorty took a rather threatening step forward to claim his lost property—and anyway, Mr Olderfleet appeared at that moment. She let Shorty have the yo-yo and Gowso sighed with relief.

Wait'll she counts her fish! he was thinking.

Roll-call had finished and mental arithmetic had just begun when a girl came in with a piece of paper. She walked straight to Mr Olderfleet's desk and said, 'A note for you to read out, sir. It's about the bazaar, there's a prize for the class that brings in the most things. Our class has twenty-five tins already.'

People immediately abandoned their pencils in order to listen properly. This was important. It was a well-known and rather shocking fact that they were driving about in a new school minibus which still had to be paid for. The bazaar was the latest attempt to get the school out of debt. Food stalls, plant stalls, toy stalls and white elephant stalls were to be set up in the assembly hall.

But Mr Olderfleet did not seem to be interested in the bazaar. He glared at the girl with the note as if she'd spoken to him in Morse code.

'Don't you think you should knock before you come into a room?'

'Yes, Mr Olderfleet.'

'So go outside and try again.'

This time when the girl came into the room after knocking, she didn't take her eyes off the floor, and she was blushing. The whole incident proved once more to Penny Brown that Mr Olderfleet didn't like

81

ildren at all—in which case, she thought, he would be far better off with a job in the bank, counting money.

Eventually he decided to tell the class about the note.

'Attention please. It seems that this bazaar will be held at the end of the week. Bring in anything you can for the various stalls— tins and things, white elephants, books in good condition. I'm quite sure there must be a tin of baked beans or a white elephant lurking about your house, Noel Alexander?'

For once Shorty didn't quite know what to say. There was hardly room in his house for a cat never mind an elephant, no matter what colour it was.

'What about you, Philip McGowan?' said Mr Olderfleet. 'Have you a tin of pears or stewed prunes locked away in a cupboard?'

Poor old Gowso shifted about in his seat with a Why-is-he-picking-on-me-for-a-tin-of-stewed-prunes look on his face.

'Oh well,' sighed Mr Olderfleet. 'Do what you can, you lot. This note says that the class who collects most will win a trip to the stars.'

'The stars?' said Shorty, pointing to the roof. 'You mean . . . up there?'

'No. I mean the local planetarium, and I'd say this class has no chance. Eyes down—next question!'

By the end of lunchtime that day, everybody was talking about the Great Bazaar. No matter where you went there were giant bullseye posters reminding you that the money-target was an incredible five thousand pounds. The assembly hall now looked more like the town's market than the serious place where they all sat on the floor and sang hymns. Gowso wondered whether the headmaster knew about the balloons hanging from the ceiling.

A giant chart in the main hall

recorded the value of what each class brought in for the sale. Jimmy Zest and company saw it on their way to dinners, and it almost put them off their food. One class had contributed nothing so far—their own.

'Nothing,' said Penny Brown, aghast. 'A big round O. Absolute zero. We are a disgrace!'

They discussed the problem of the bazaar on the way home.

'I bet he thinks we're useless,' said Penny Brown, referring to Mr Olderfleet. 'He probably thinks our class will bring in hardly any tins at all! I think we should bring in a ton of baked beans and sicken him.'

'We have none,' said, Shorty. 'Knuckles eats them cold out of the tin.'

And he probably uses his fingers, thought Mandy Taylor. 'Come on, Shorty,' she said. 'You must have something in your larder, everybody's got tins of *something*, for heaven's sake.'

Jimmy Zest had been quiet until now.

'If everybody has tins, why don't we

ask them for donations?'

'You mean—go round the doors? Just walk up somebody's path and ask them for a tin out of their cupboard?'

Obviously Mandy didn't think it was good manners to beg like that. Support came from Gowso, who said that there were probably laws against it, leading to imprisonment.

They had arrived by now at the shops, where Penny Brown saw that here was a chance to test Jimmy Zest and his latest scheme.

'Right, Zesty—go into the grocer's and ask him if he'll give you a tin for our minibus bazaar. I bet he'll throw you out for scrounging.'

To her astonishment, the challenge was accepted. Jimmy Zest strode boldly into the grocer's with Shorty on one side of him and Legweak on the other. Penny and Mandy waited outside with Gowso, who had just decided to walk on home by himself when the other three reappeared.

Shorty's hand was in the air, triumphantly. 'Catch, Gowso. Tin of corned beef!'

It was indeed a tin of corned beef. Gowso examined it as if it was a fake.

Legweak rubbed his hands together, eager for more action.

'We'll get millions of tins, dead easy. Where to now, Zesty?'

Jimmy Zest, the General, held up a restraining hand. He saw clearly that the impulse of enthusiasm was not quite enough for this operation—they needed planning time to think.

'Meet in my garage after tea,' he said impressively, 'at six-fifteen precisely.'

*     *     *

By twenty to seven they were almost ready.

Jimmy Zest stood in his garage, clipboard in one hand, pencil in the other, and wrote:

CORNED BEEF—1 TIN

carefully on a page.

At his side Legweak wore the advertising boards which Jimmy Zest had hastily prepared. The front board

said: SUPPORT OUR SCHOOL BAZAAR, the back board, PLEASE GIVE GENEROUSLY. You could see Legweak's happy face poking out at the top and the tips of his shoes underneath—the rest of him was hidden.

Knuckles had charge of the wheelbarrow. A rather nervous Mandy Taylor practised her questioning technique on Gowso, while Penny Brown, at the back of the garage, could hardly take her eyes off Shorty.

He was wearing a bone round his neck on a piece of string. At least, it looked like bone, and it was the most ridiculous thing Penny Brown had ever seen. 'OK, Shorty, I give up, what is it?'

'What's what?'

'*That!*' Penny touched it quickly. There was no telling where Shorty had picked it up.

'Lucky charm,' said Shorty.

'Where did you get it?'

'Great white shark.'

'OK, Shorty, forget it. Don't tell a friend if you don't want to.'

Shorty relented. Penny Brown was one of his favourite people, after all.

'All right, I'll tell you, but it's a secret.'

'I'll never tell,' whispered Penny.

'It's the inside bone of a giant goldfish. Our cat ate the gold bits and this is the rest.'

'Is it!' Penny Brown raised a foot furiously. 'Pull that leg as well, Shorty. It plays "Jingle Bells"!'

Meanwhile, the others had already started out on the Great Collection. They all followed Knuckles and the rattling tin of corned beef in the barrow down the street as far as Mrs Hawthorne's house, where Mandy cleared her throat and explained nicely why they were here.

'Just one tin if you have anything to spare, please, Mrs Hawthorne.'

Would it work? Mrs Hawthorne stared at the odd group of people gathered round her doorstep. She looked twice at Knuckles and the almost-empty wheelbarrow and Legweak turned his back so that she could read his other side.

'Wait there a moment, Mandy,' she said.

Three tins! Peaches, rice pudding and spaghetti hoops!

What a start, they could hardly believe it. Knuckles charged down the road with Shorty in the wheelbarrow (shouting, 'Planet Arium here we come!') and Legweak beat his chest—or rather, his advertising boards—with the palms of his hands, and howled like Tarzan calling the elephants. Penny congratulated Mandy and even Gowso smiled.

The solemn Jimmy Zest cradled his clipboard. 'Come on, everybody, we've got work to do.'

Soon the barrow was three parts full. It was as if people took a look at Legweak and were hypnotized into giving generously. Even Mr and Mrs Burns, two old-age pensioners, saw them passing and came out with four tins, including red salmon.

'Red salmon!' declared Mandy Taylor. 'I mean, it only costs a *fortune.*'

Presently the group of collectors and their creaking wheelbarrow came to the finest house in the neighbourhood, a house so big that it had eight windows in the roof and two-metre pillars at the cast-iron double gates. And here, they paused. There could be no doubt that this was the dwelling place of someone who had cupboards galore, all stacked with more tins than she would ever use: Mrs Cricklewood-Holmes, the neighbourhood millionaire, lived here. Mrs Cricklewood-Holmes liked her privacy. One Christmas—so ran the local gossip—she had set her brute of a Dobermann dog on innocent carol singers. And once, due to a case of mistaken identity, she had caught Jimmy Zest and his collectors in her garden. They wouldn't like to be caught there again. Small wonder that they dithered at her gate.

Gowso broke the silence.

'She wears a fox round her neck,

you know.'

'A fox?' Knuckles was quite startled. 'Round her *neck?*'

'A whole fox?' Legweak echoed. 'You're wired to the moon, Gowso.'

'Yes, a fox,' said Gowso, who didn't enjoy criticism. 'I'm telling you, its feet hang down her back in church and its eyes keep looking at you.'

'Is it alive?' Knuckles asked rapturously. He'd never heard of such a thing.

Penny Brown had had enough of this.

'Look, it's a wrap, a fur wrap. They wore them in the olden days. Are we going to ask her for tins or do we stand here all night?'

Mandy Taylor was about to insist that they shouldn't bother, but Shorty had the gate open for Knuckles to take the barrow through.

The gravel crunched under their feet all the way up the drive and it was not a heartening sound. And when Shorty rapped the heavy knocker the whole house boomed and a dog started to howl.

'Guard dog,' whispered Legweak. 'Remember it? Watch it doesn't eat you, Gowso.'

When Mrs Cricklewood-Holmes came to the door she was not wearing her fox. Her rather lifeless, watery eyes and puckered mouth reduced Mandy Taylor to silence—but the valiant Shorty stepped forward one pace.

'Missus, have you any spare tins? We're saving up for a minibus. Legweak, turn round and let her read your back. And white elephants, we take them as well if you have some.'

Actually, Shorty had not the slightest idea what a white elephant consisted of, but he felt sure that Cricklewood-Holmesy had plenty.

They were bitterly disappointed. Mrs Cricklewood-Holmes—or Scrooge's twin sister, as Penny Brown called her once they were safely out of earshot—gave them a rusty tin of treacle and a peculiar flat box, and told them to shut the gate after them.

As soon as they were out of sight Knuckles stopped the wheelbarrow and the others urged Jimmy Zest to open the flat box.

'I mean, she only gave them away to get rid of us!' said the indignant Mandy Taylor.

The lid was dusty. After some rubbing Jimmy Zest managed to read a word. 'It says FIGS.'

'Figs?'

'Or fags?' suggested Legweak.

'They're probably blue-mouldy,' said Mandy.

Jimmy Zest opened the seal and poked about with his fingers.

'They're sticky,' he said. 'Wait a minute—here's something. Hey, take a look at this!'

Gowso, stuck at the back, could tell that it was something rather special, perhaps the well-preserved body of a giant tarantula in the age-old figs.

But Jimmy Zest had a card in his hand. Five glittering coins had been taped to the card. Shorty pressed closer for a look.

'What are they, Zesty, two-pence pieces?'

'No way. This one's got Queen Victoria's head on it, see? These are sovereigns. Old coins. These are real gold.'

Gowso's eyebrows shot up. He mumbled, 'Jeepers creepers.'

Mandy Taylor whispered, 'My mummy has one of those on a chain and it's worth over two hundred pounds.'

Seven silent heads did the same sum.

Even Shorty got it right. Five gold coins, one thousand pounds. Legweak saw his picture in the local paper under a giant headline, SCHOOLBOY FINDS FORTUNE IN FIGS.

'I am telling you,' said Shorty, 'we are in the big time now.' He kissed the bone round his neck. This was a lucky day.

Penny Brown took the card from Jimmy Zest and read out the words:

*Couldn't get out to the shops, love, these will have to do. Hope you'll be up and about soon. Merry Xmas, my darling Rachel. All my love, Grandpa*

'What about these coins?' asked Legweak. 'Who owns them now?'

Nobody knew, not even Gowso, who usually had legal opinions about that kind of thing.

'It's a pity there isn't one each,' said Knuckles.

'What?' Penny Brown was shocked. 'You mean to *keep* . . .?'

'Certainly. They were given to us,

veren't they?'

'They were not indeed, Nicholas Alexander. One thousand pounds! Are you crazy?'

'So what do we do, then?' asked Legweak.

'There's only one thing we can do,' said Jimmy Zest, clipping the coins to his board. 'They have to go back. Otherwise we'll get into trouble. Any volunteers?'

There were no volunteers. Gowso actually stepped backwards. 'I'll take them back,' said Jimmy Zest.

He was gone for about three minutes, and returned to face a burst of questions from Penny Brown.

'Well? What did she say?'

'Nothing.'

'Didn't she say who Rachel was?'

'No.'

'Didn't she say thank you?'

'No.'

'Huh,' said Penny Brown.

After a few minutes more of collecting, the mountain of groceries in the barrow was so huge that avalanches of tins occurred. The methodical

Jimmy Zest informed the company th
they now had a grand total of on
hundred and fifty-three items,
including the original tin of corned
beef.

'Just wait'll he sees that little lot!'
said Penny Brown, thinking of Mr
Olderfleet.

\* \* \*

'Right!'

Mr Olderfleet tapped his desk with a
metre rule.

'The moment of truth has arrived.
How many tins have we managed to
scrape up? Thirty-three, one each?
Twenty-five? A baker's dozen?'

He sounded like an auctioneer.
Jimmy Zest rose to his feet, clutching a
white sheet of paper.

'Mr Olderfleet, we have twenty-nine
tins . . .'

'Twenty-nine! Well, could be worse,
I suppose.'

'Yes, sir, but that's twenty-nine tins
of baked beans. We also have thirty-
four tins of soup, twenty-eight pears,

enty-two peaches, fourteen tinned
eas both marrowfat and garden,
twelve tins of spaghetti hoops and ten
cans of fish including red salmon. We
have more than one each of macaroni
cheese, asparagus, mandarin segments,
tapioca pudding and quite a few more.
Sir, altogether one hundred and eighty-
seven tins plus some bottles, one
coconut, and twenty items in packets
including long-grained rice from the
East.'

And with that speech off his ches
Jimmy Zest signalled to the Alexander
twins who left the classroom and
sprinted outside.

The wheelbarrow had come to
school that morning. The astonished
Mr Olderfleet simply gaped as Shorty
and Knuckles wheeled it in from the
corridor.

'No white elephants, sir,' Shorty
confessed, 'they must be died-out.'

'You mean extinct.'

'You're right. Extinct.'

Each class had to take their tins over
to the assembly hall, which was already
packed with busy people, but all work
stopped when the contingent trooped
in from Mr Olderfleet's class—behind
their full wheelbarrow. Knuckles and
Shorty began to chant, 'We are the
Champions!' until Mr Olderfleet
threatened to send them back to class.

Penny and Mandy organized a
moving chain of groceries to the
appropriate stalls. Up on the stage
Legweak entertained Gowso by
juggling two tins of baked beans and
the coconut—until he saw the

admaster enter the hall, and stuffed them up his jumper in fright.

When the hall was quiet, Mr Wilson spoke.

'Some children from this school collected round the doors yesterday. I cannot think of anything more guaranteed to give us all a bad name. I want those people in my office—immediately. All of them!'

Flute! A great finger of guilt pointed down from the sky straight at Penny Brown. Two cans and a coconut fell out of Legweak's jumper as he made for the corridor, where he met Gowso. Gowso had lost the will to live—his feet wanted to turn round and run away with him in the opposite direction. Mandy Taylor bit her lip and said, 'I didn't think it was right to beg like that. Not really.'

'This is your fault as usual, Jimmy Zest,' Penny Brown said with feeling.

When at last the company had shuffled into Mr Wilson's office, they saw Mrs Cricklewood-Holmes standing there.

And she was wearing her fox! We are

really, really for it, thought Gowso.

'That's him.' She pointed to Jimmy Zest. 'That's the boy, there.'

Mr Wilson frowned fiercely. 'They should not have collected round the doors, it is not our policy, Mrs Cricklewood-Holmes. You have every right to complain.'

'That is *not* why I am here, Headmaster.'

'Oh . . .?' Mr Wilson seemed as surprised as everybody else when she set five shining coins on his desk.

'I gave the children a box of figs. Actually I had no idea it was so old—I don't believe the thing was ever opened. Well, these coins were inside, and . . . well, it brought back such memories. I had forgotten, you see. It was such a . . . a sad time.'

Penny Brown was convinced that tears came into Cricklewood-Holmesy's eyes. Why should that be, she wondered?

Mr Wilson, still puzzled, hastily gave her a seat and Shorty took a sideways step to see the back legs of her fox.

'These children returned the coins to

me, and I applaud honesty, Headmaster, there isn't enough of it nowadays. So I've come to a decision. You shall have these sovereigns for your fund.'

'What?' Mr Wilson gave a startled little jump. 'No, indeed, we could not accept . . .'

'You shall accept, that's why I am here. I can think of no better use for them and I absolutely insist, Headmaster!'

Even the fox twitched aggressively. Mandy Taylor felt sorry for the poor thing. She didn't like foxes much but she didn't think it was right to turn them into scarves.

Jimmy Zest made a short thank-you speech on behalf of the school, then Mr Wilson bustled them out of his office as if he was glad to be rid of them.

Gowso felt limp, like something squeezed out of a tube.

'We were lucky, I'm telling you. If she hadn't been there he would have murdered us.'

Shorty produced the disgusting

bone which had brought him luck these last few days, and to Gowso's consternation, gave it a kiss right in front of Mandy Taylor.

'She's really quite nice, isn't she,' said Mandy, referring to Mrs Cricklewood-Holmes.

'Tell that to her fox,' mumbled Legweak.

\*     \*     \*

In the afternoon a note came round the school with some important information. Mr Olderfleet smiled before he read it out.

'The class which collected most for the school bazaar, and which wins the trip to the planetarium was . . . mine. Well done, you people.'

In the good old days, when Miss Quick was in charge, they would have cheered. But they didn't dare.

Penny Brown walked home from school with Jimmy Zest that day. He explained that two greenfly, born at six o'clock in the morning, could be grandparents by six o'clock that night.

Big deal, Zesty, thought Penny Brown. They ended up in the graveyard. Jimmy Zest scanned the tombstones, looking for a particular name.

'Come on, Zesty—you'll be in the graveyard soon enough, for goodness' sake.'

'I won't. I'm being cremated.'

Typical, thought Penny Brown. Jimmy Zest had his future all planned out.

Eventually he found what he was looking for. The stone carried this inscription:

**VICTORIA RACHEL
CRICKLEWOOD-HOLMES
BORN 18th June 1978
DIED BOXING DAY 1993**
*She Was God's Lovely Loan*

'Rachel was her daughter,' Jimmy Zest said. 'I thought she might be. I wondered why they didn't open the figs. She must have been too ill that Christmas for presents and things.'

Life is really peculiar, thought Penny Brown. Yesterday she'd started out collecting up tins, now here she was in the graveyard almost in tears thinking of Mrs Cricklewood-Holmes and her poor sick daughter up in the big house. At Christmas time, too.

They closed the graveyard gate, and Penny decided to talk about something else.

'Zesty, do you know anything about that bone round Shorty's neck? I think he's getting worse, you know. He says it's from a giant goldfish but where would Shorty get a goldfish? Anyway, there's no such thing as a giant goldfish. Mind you, Mandy's are quite . . .'

She didn't finish saying the word 'big'. An incredible thought had just invaded her whole brain.

'Oh my stars! Zesty. I *know.*'

The chipped gnome . . . the yellow yo-yo . . .

'It was one of Mandy's! Oh, she'll be furious! And then . . . he probably fed it to their *cat*!'

Jimmy Zest said nothing at all, but that was quite enough in the circumstances.

'A nineteen-year-old goldfish and he fed it to his cat, and now he wears it as a *neck* ornament!'

'It's of sentimental value,' said Jimmy Zest. 'That was the first fish he ever actually caught. You don't have to tell, Penelope.'

'What do you mean, Zesty, I don't

have to *tell?*'

Of course she had to tell, it was her duty to pass on such information to a friend and she was heading straight for Mandy's house this very second!

## 5

## *The Worst Goalie on Earth*

It was ten o'clock on an unusually cold morning in April, and a biting wind swept across the open spaces of the park. The weather was not at all good for football.

All the same, Jimmy Zest stood in the bandstand with a ball trapped under his foot. He had an important announcement to make to his listeners.

'OK, here is the latest news. We are the ALL-STARS, that's our name on the official form. Mandy Taylor is in goal. Gowso, you're centre back. Shorty and Legweak—midfield. Knuckles is the All-Star striker and, Penelope, you're a wingman.'

'Wing*person*, Zesty, if you don't mind. And which wing?'

'Both wings, we're only allowed six players.'

Huh, thought Penny Brown, he must

think I can fly.

They were not alone in the park that morning. The place was full of little groups practising their passing and dribbling skills and scheming for victory. Football fever had gripped the neighbourhood and it was always the same at this time of year because of the Six-a-Sides.

The staff of the local leisure centre organized the tournament. Mums and dads came to watch and there were photographs of the star players in the weekly paper. The winning team received a shield and medals. If *your* team won the Sixes you felt that people noticed you walking down the street, and you seemed to stand a little bit taller in the chippie queue.

And this year, Jimmy Zest had entered a team. They stood in front of him now, his All-Stars. Shorty had a question.

'What position are you playing, Zesty?'

'I won't actually be playing,' said Jimmy Zest, who was not much good at football, 'I'm the manager.'

He felt entitled to be manager, his name was on the application form.

Then Mandy Taylor came out with her bombshell. 'I won't be playing either,' she said.

Now to win the Six-a-Sides you needed a strong team—for example, like last year's winners The Elm Street Strollers captained by Knuckles's old rival, Maurice Baimes. And the All-Stars *did* have quite a strong team. True, Gowso wasn't brilliant, because he was afraid of the ball, but the others could all play, and in recent months Mandy Taylor, who did ballet and gymnastics, had developed into a marvellous goalkeeper.

Knuckles turned round and looked her square in the eyes. 'Listen you, you're playing.'

'I am not. There is nothing in the rules of the country that says I have to play football if I don't want to.'

Jimmy Zest tapped the official entry form. 'You have to play, your name's on the official list I gave to the organizers.'

'Is it? Well I do not play football with

goldfish stealers. I do not play football with people who feed my dead animals to their cat, so you can forget it, Zesty.'

Away she went. Mandy Taylor walked out on them, taking small steps with great dignity.

Even Penny Brown was astonished by this turn of events, although she quickly realized that she should have seen this coming. Mandy had *not* whisked herself into a tantrum when she heard the dreadful facts about her dead fish. Instead she had saved up her revenge until this crucial moment, when she knew it would really hurt.

The others were left to puzzle over the same question: how were the All-Stars going to beat Baimes and his lot without a goalkeeper?

Knuckles saw the answer immediately. 'Well that's it, then. You'll have to be goalie, Zesty.'

'I can't, I'm the manager.'

'We don't need a manager, Zesty!' Penny Brown declared with some force. We need a goalie and you're it. Come on, let's play.'

In view of the sudden emergency,

they decided that they had better give their new goalkeeper some shooting-in practice. Gowso and Legweak put down their coats for posts, and Jimmy Zest stood between them.

He looked quite impressive, standing there in a crouch. Shorty stepped up, and scored. Penny Brown stepped up, and scored. Legweak hit a shot with his left foot and Jimmy Zest watched it slowly dribble past him into a corner.

'Ah, for crying out loud, Zesty, will you *move*,' said Knuckles. 'You have to move if you're going to save the ball. *Dive.*'

After that they decided to practise corner kicks. This was Penny Brown's job, since she could cross a ball as accurately as any of them. She could also do banana kicks because, Gowso claimed, she had bandy legs.

Penny delivered a high, hanging ball into the penalty area, where it dropped towards Gowso, the tall centre back.

'Go for it, Gowso,' yelled Knuckles. 'Head it away!'

And Gowso, seeing the ball dropping through the air like a big wet pudding, cleverly ducked out of the way. Shorty trapped the ball and tapped it past the motionless, crouching Jimmy Zest.

Knuckles hung his head in despair.

'Why did you not head the ball, Gowso?'

'That thing would knock you out, that's why.'

'But it's only an ordinary football.'

Gowso was muttering something about not suffering brain damage when other voices made themselves heard— and they were not friendly.

'Oi! throw away your crutches, Alexander.'

'Go see a vet and he'll straighten your feet.'

Maurice Baimes had arrived with some of his team, and they were looking for trouble.

'Easy!' they shouted. 'Easy, easy, easy!'

'Just ignore the big baboon, Knuckles,' advised Penny Brown.

She knew it was impossible. Neither Knuckles nor Shorty was capable of ignoring anybody who taunted them, let alone Baimes and his lot. There had always been bad feeling between them, especially since that Strong Stomach contest.

They headed towards the enemy as if drawn by magnets.

'What are you looking at, Baimes?'

'Not much.'

'Spying on us?'

'Nothing to see.'

'Wait'll we get at you next week.'

'What do you lot know about football,' said Baimes. 'Is the ball round or square?'

Until that moment Penny Brown had not intended to say anything at all, but she sometimes suffered from fits of temper, and there was one coming on right now.

'We know as much as you know, turnip head,' she said with feeling.

Maurice Baimes gave one of his insolent little smiles as he backed away with his friends, Gnome and Billy Parks.

'Ten-nil. We'll hammer you. See if we don't hammer you ten-nil!' As the Elm Street Strollers marched away down the tree-lined avenue of the park, they put their hands above their heads and started up a chant which could be heard a long way off: 'Champions!'— *clap-clap-clap*—'Champions!'—*clap-clap-clap*.

For a moment or two Knuckles stared after them as if they'd put a spell on him. The fact is that he had just realized what the most painful thing in the world would be—to lose in the Six-a-Sides against the Strollers.

'OK, Zesty,' he said grimly. 'You're going to learn how to dive!'

Legweak, Shorty and Knuckles sat on the wall outside the chip shop.

The chippy wall was one of their favourite resting perches on account of the gorgeous smells which occasionally drifted by. Since the lads were usually penniless, sitting on the chippy wall amounted to a form of self-torture.

Something else bothered them on this particular day. It was Friday evening already, and Jimmy Zest's goalkeeping had not improved. True, he could now dive for the ball, but only after it was in the net. Legweak said he'd be quicker in action replay.

Presently Maurice Baimes walked by with a fish supper steaming in his right hand. Enemies or not, Shorty could not resist the smell.

'Give us a chip, Baimes.'

'No.'

'Keep your chips, keep your chips,' shouted Shorty.

Baimes selected a particularly fat chip and joyfully tossed it to the

116

ground at their feet.

'There, eat that one.'

Knuckles hopped off the wall and flung it after him.

'Ten-nil!' laughed Baimes. And he squashed the chip with his heel.

Five minutes later Penny Brown and Jimmy Zest arrived with news from the leisure centre.

'Guess who's coming to the tournament!' cried Penny. 'The mayor! It said so on the notice board.'

'I should think so indeed,' said Shorty, as if he'd been expecting Her Majesty the Queen.

'And,' said Jimmy Zest, 'we've drawn The Choir in the first round.'

A pause occurred while they did some thinking. Every year the cathedral choir entered a team for the Sixes. Knuckles tried hard to convince himself that a bunch of singers shouldn't be too hard to beat, but he didn't quite manage it. The Choir had Mavis Purvis on their side.

In the classroom, Mavis Purvis was the quietest little mouse there could be—Miss Quick had always been on at her to speak up, and she had not dared open her mouth since the arrival of Mr Olderfleet. But when she stepped out to play football, Mavis Purvis changed. For as long as the game lasted, she ran about the field popping up here, there and everywhere to head goals, make crosses and deliver tackles as if her legs were made of rubber.

She would have to be watched.

While such thoughts occupied the minds of his team, Jimmy Zest had not been idle. He had quickly scribbled a note on a piece of scrap paper from the litter bin.

'As manager of the All-Stars,' he said gravely, 'I think we should deliver this note immediately.' They crowded round to see what it said and whom it was for.

*Dear Amanda,*
*We are sorry for borrowing your ornamental carp. We deeply regret its death which was a complete accident and we have respectfully buried the bone.*
*Perhaps you would consider*

*playing goalkeeper for the All-*
*Stars in front of our mayor.*
  *Yours sincerely,*

They liked it.

'It's beautifully written, Zesty,' said Penny Brown. 'I think we should all take it to her door right now.'

First they had to remove the fish bone from Shorty's neck. When this was accomplished, in spite of his protests, they wrapped it in an empty crisp packet from the litter bin and scraped a shallow grave in the gritty soil. Shorty marked the grave with a large stone so that he could dig it up later if need be; then they set off eagerly for Mandy Taylor's house.

Her father's Mercedes was parked in the drive.

'Now listen, Shorty,' warned Penny Brown as they squeezed by, 'be careful what you say. You're in the wrong, so eat humble pie.'

Shorty nodded obediently. He was always ready for any kind of pie.

Mandy herself answered the door. It was quite clear from her feet that she had no intention of coming out, for she was wearing her multicoloured indoor bootees from Lapland.

Jimmy Zest, manager, handed her the note, which she duly read.

'No. I'm not playing.'

'You're playing!' snapped Knuckles. 'Your name's down.'

'Tough,' said Mandy, who did not intend to be bullied at her own front door.

'You don't want to play against Baimes,' said Knuckles, *'that's* what it is. He's your boyfriend.'

'He is *not.*'

'He is, you were dancing with him at the youth club last year.'

'I was not dancing *with* him, we were dancing back-to-back.'

'You were dancing front-to-front,' Shorty joined in, 'and you blew him kisses.'

Mandy Taylor looked right through Shorty without speaking. What she was thinking could not be said out loud.

Then Penny Brown spoke very seriously.

'Well, Mandy, I don't think it's fair. You're punishing me too if you don't play and I had nothing to do with kidnapping your goldfish. And the mayor's coming. I won't speak to you again if you don't play.'

'Don't speak then,' said Mandy, and shut the door in their faces.

That was that. Shorty wanted to

shout, 'You're a balloon,' through the letter box but Penny Brown told him quite bluntly not to be so stupid. They retreated quietly into the street.

Knuckles was resigned. The following day they had to play against The Choir and the Strollers with probably the worst goalie on planet Earth.

'Too bad,' he said, 'we'll just have to do the best we can without her.'

'OK, everybody—get a good night's sleep,' said Jimmy Zest, just like a manager.

# 6

## *The All-Stars Do or Die!*

Her Worship the Mayor, four referees, two members of the St John Ambulance Brigade, over seventy football players, a photographer from the weekly paper, scores of mums and dads and eight of Gowso's cousins—all these people and many more gathered near the leisure centre that Saturday morning in order to participate in the Six-a-Sides.

Penny Brown arrived in the car and didn't want to get out when she saw the crowds.

'Penny,' said her mother, 'go and score some goals and none of your nonsense.'

'Mummy, it's not easy scoring goals, you know. We're going to get knocked out in the first round.'

Mrs Brown leaned across her daughter and opened the door.

'You can but try—do or die,' she said poetically.

After running about for a while, Penny felt better. She saw Mandy standing alone on one of the touchlines and she was dressed in a green duffelcoat, woollen hat and gloves—like a spectator, in fact. Penny ignored her. They still weren't speaking.

The next two All-Stars to arrive were Legweak and Gowso, who went for a jog to keep warm. They met Knuckles and Shorty, already stripped for action.

At first Knuckles did not suffer from big-match tension; then he saw the fat lady with the gold chain round her neck sitting at the PRIZES table. He noticed the medals, and the cup, the heart-shaped wooden shield embossed with silver circles, and his body tingled with excitement.

Once he bumped into Maurice Baimes and they gave one another a quick nod.

No more insults. It was down to skill and stamina. Baimes looked anxious, too.

Jimmy Zest, Manager, at last managed to get all his players together in one place for a pre-match pep talk.

'Look here,' he said, chasing away most of Gowso's cousins, 'this is a copy of the complete draw for the tournament. You'll see we've got a bye after two rounds. Win two games and we're in the final. OK everybody?'

Nobody was OK. Gowso actually felt sick. Someone in the distance called out for the All-Stars to get ready and Shorty wished they could blindfold the opposition.

\*     \*     \*

As far as Penny Brown was concerned, the first match simply started in a blur. She felt the silence, saw her mum's face, saw Gowso's cousins leaping about like caged ferrets, heard the whistle—and the ball came straight towards her as if she'd called its name! She was tackled hard and Mavis Purvis came away with the ball.

'*Penneee!*' somebody shouted, a man's voice. She picked herself up, nerves all gone.

Luckily Mavis Purvis couldn't win the game on her own. Knuckles shadowed her everywhere, and soon the All-Stars' forwards found that they had lots of room. Late in the first period of ten minutes, Penny gathered the ball in her own half, ran with it up the wing and pushed a lovely ball into Legweak's path. As The Choir goalie came out, Legweak squared the ball to Shorty, who hit the back of an empty net.

Oh, the scenes! Legweak did a cartwheel, Shorty shouted 'one-nil' in case the referee couldn't count, and some of Gowso's cousins invaded the pitch.

Early in the second half Legweak got a goal, then Knuckles chipped one in for their third. When the whistle went, Mavis Purvis immediately held out her hand to Knuckles. Penny thought it was very sporting of her.

As they came off the pitch they saw the captain of the People-Eaters being led away by his dad. The boy was sobbing his heart out.

'What's the matter with *him*?' said Legweak.

They soon found out, and it wasn't good news. Maurice Baimes and the Strollers had destroyed the poor People-Eaters eleven-nil.

\*　　　\*　　　\*

Mr Pinkerton, the referee, blew his whistle and started the second round game between the All-Stars and The Scouts: and disaster struck within seconds. One of The Scouts hit a high ball far into the All-Star's half.

Their centre back stood underneath it, waiting.

'Head it away, Gowso!' Knuckles screamed.

Perhaps Gowso really did intend to head that ball, but it didn't matter, his eyes were shut at the time and he didn't even get close. Behind Gowso, on the goal-line, Jimmy Zest was tying a shoe-lace. Legweak could hardly believe it.

'*Zesty!*'

Too late. Jimmy Zest saw the ball when it was past him and in the back of the net.

Knuckles nearly had a fit.

'Wake up! Boy, you're some goalie, Zesty. Whose side are you on?'

And for a moment, Penny Brown panicked. They had the worst goalie in the world and a centre back who was afraid of brain damage, how could they *possibly* win?

From then on, Knuckles took control of the game. Every time he got the ball he beat at least two players, then distributed the ball to Shorty, Legweak or Penny. In this way the All-Stars took a two-one lead by half-time.

Late in the second half, Penny got the shock of her life. She had just taken a pass from Gowso, only to find everybody covered. She didn't know what to do with the ball.

'Go with it yourself, Penny Brown,' said a man's voice. '*Run!*'

Flute! She suddenly realized it was Mr Olderfleet. What was *he* doing here?

Off she went, feet flying. The Scouts, afraid of Legweak and Shorty, hung back, expecting her to pass.

But she didn't pass. The goalie rushed off his line, sensing the danger, screaming for cover as Penny paused, leaned back, and gently lobbed the ball over his head with perfect weight.

It crossed the line on the third bounce.

'Oh beautiful, beautiful skill!' Shorty cried out to the heavens in ecstasy.

Her mum had seen it happen! And Mr Olderfleet! What Penny Brown felt at that moment was true bliss. Shorty spoiled it a little by heaving her off her feet with a bear hug.

The All-Stars beat The Scouts three-one. They were celebrating when the word came through that the Strollers had thrashed the Hilltown Stingers by nine goals to two.

Maurice Baimes was in the final, too.

\*       \*       \*

As the crowd gathered round one pitch for the only remaining match—the

Strollers v the All-Stars—Jimmy Zest searched among the beaten teams until he found the person he was looking for.

She was changing. Jimmy Zest helped Mavis Purvis into her tracksuit.

'I think you're a very good footballer, Mavis,' he said.

'Thanks, Zesty.'

'How would you like a transfer?'

Mavis tucked her pigtail into her tracksuit top without giving an answer. Jimmy Zest and his schemes were notorious.

'I mean it. Baimes and his lot will walk over us, you know that's true, Mavis.'

'But I play for The Choir.'

'Not any more, they're out of it. With you and Knuckles in the same team we've got a chance. I'll substitute Gowso.'

In her heart, Mavis Purvis loved football. And yet she hated controversy.

'I'll have to ask my team, Zesty. If they agree, I'll do it.'

'Well hurry up,' said Jimmy Zest.

'We haven't got much time.'

*　　　*　　　*

Out on the pitch the two teams were in separate huddles. Mr Pinkerton stood in the centre circle with a foot resting on the ball and the whistle in his mouth.

Knuckles was talking grimly—already he'd lost the toss against Maurice Baimes.

'This is it, we're getting stuck in here, no slacking. Zesty, you stay awake. Mavis, you stay near me and take Baimes if he gets past me. Let's go. We die out here.'

Legweak's eyes shone with the light of battle, but that talk about dying made Gowso quite glad that his manager had substituted him.

A short blast of the whistle brought both teams into the middle for the referee's friendly chat.

'Well done, all of you, you've done extremely well to get to the final. In the event of a tie, the team with the most goals overall will win. Remember that

the game is not only a
however, it's about enjoy
well. Good luck to you.'

Penny Brown stood
literally shaking. It was
she was thinking, for M
talk that way, he was only the referee.
Of course it mattered who won—if
people didn't care who won, games
would have died out years ago!

She noticed the skin stretched tightly
over Maurice Baimes's eager face. *He*
cared who won.

Excitement stirred in her tummy like
a living thing. And then the whistle
happened.

The game began quietly.

It was the Strollers who first
managed to maintain possession for
any length of time. After a few passes
in midfield, Billy Parks found Maurice
Baimes with a long ball into the All-
Stars goalmouth. Baimes slipped
Legweak's tackle, steadied himself, and
hit a right foot shot from close range.

Jimmy Zest put out his hands as if to
warm them at the fire, and the ball
went between his legs.

were one down. Knuckles ...d his head in agony and ...dered if there were nine more to ...ome.

From the centre, the ball went to Knuckles, to Legweak, to Shorty going forward.

'Get rid of it, Shorty!' yelled Legweak.

Baimes was closing in. As the tackle arrived, Shorty swung his leg so hard that he fell off his feet and the ball looped across the Strollers' goal. Mavis Purvis rose, she flew, she met that ball sweetly with her forehead and Gnome, in goal, had no chance.

'One-all!' screamed Shorty.

Two minutes later Baimes beat Knuckles in midfield and left him standing. Penny Brown tried to barge him off the ball but she simply bounced off him and fell down.

Baimes had the goalie to beat. A cry sounded out from the touchline. 'Come out and meet him, Jimmy Zest!' Penny Brown realized that this was Mr Olderfleet shouting his head off, and she was quite shocked.

Jimmy Zest snorted like a pig as Baimes closed in to shoot. Then he jumped up and down, clucking like a farmyard hen and waggling his elbows. Another player, accustomed to normal goalkeepers, might have taken his eye off the ball; Maurice Baimes calmly swerved to his right and neatly side-footed the ball past Jimmy Zest—who by this time was baaing like a sheep.

The referee blew his whistle.

'Half-time. And you,'—he meant Jimmy Zest—'this is a game of football, not Old MacDonald's Farm, so cut out the animal noises. Change ends!'

At half-time, which was only just long enough to suck an officially provided orange slice, Jimmy Zest led the All-Stars to that part of the touchline where Mandy Taylor was standing.

'We need you,' he said simply. 'You have to do goal for us.'

Mandy was already stripping off her duffelcoat—it wasn't necessary for Shorty to fall on his knees begging like a dog. Penny embraced her and they both had tears in their eyes.

Soon there was excitement at both ends. Shorty put one over the bar from six yards and felt like killing himself. Mandy Taylor sprinted off her line to boot the ball into touch. Then Penny hit a lovely cross towards Legweak, who struck the ball on the volley. Legweak was paralysed with shock when it hit the back of the net.

Sheer luck also played a part in the next goal. After a corner kick, during a mad goalmouth scramble, the ball bobbed about like a cork on the ocean. Shorty hit the ball and it ricocheted off at least four players and over the

Strollers' line, whereupon Shorty, at his wits' end, took off on a trip round the goalposts, and finally stood still with his arms outstretched, waiting for Knuckles and Legweak to catch up and worship him.

Penny saw Mr Olderfleet screaming like a pagan from the really olden days.

'A minute to go!' he was shouting.

The All-Stars were three-two up with a minute to go! Baimes, too, realized what must be done. Collecting the ball on the left side of the pitch, he quickly made ground into the other half. Legweak couldn't catch him and left him to Knuckles, who missed with his sliding tackle.

The goal loomed large. Baimes lifted his right foot and Mavis Purvis took his legs and ball with a bone-crunching tackle.

'PENALTY!' shouted Gnome from the distant goalmouth.

'FAIR TACKLE!' yelled Shorty, and Penny Brown's heart sank. She felt hollow inside.

The referee pointed to the spot.

In this dramatic way the outcome of

the Six-a-Side tournament came down to virtually the last kick of the game, for the Elm Street Strollers only required a three-all draw to win on goal difference.

As Maurice Baimes placed the ball, Penny, like Billy Parks and Legweak, faced the opposite direction rather than face reality. A silence had come over the crowd, so she heard the soft

thud as Baimes struck the ball.

Afterwards, Mandy Taylor claimed that she didn't decide to dive just any old way—she said she had time to see the ball, time to realize that it was travelling low and to her left, time to know that she could only get it if she dived: and so she launched herself towards the moving target, caught it with hands, and slid across her goalmouth to safety.

She rose up, cuddling the ball as if it was a baby.

'I've got you,' she told it. As the referee blew his whistle she saw the exhausted face of Maurice Baimes, shattered that he hadn't blasted the ball instead of trying to place it, and she was sorry for him.

Then the Alexander twins hoisted her into the air. The others arrived, and big Gowso, like a fool, jumped on them all and toppled them into the muck.

'Will you get up, you're squashing me!' said Legweak's muffled voice at the bottom of the heap.

About two minutes later, they heard

the first rumour that they'd been disqualified.

It was true.

The All-Stars *had* been disqualified.

The organizers gathered into a private little huddle and then announced that since the All-Stars had played too many substitutes, they could not be regarded as fair winners.

The team and their manager were absolutely stunned. Poor Shorty lay flat on his back and stared up at the open sky. His eyeballs did not move. Gowso was quite worried about, him.

That was when Penny Brown began to hear an argument starting up amid all the confusion surrounding the PRIZES table. And her eyes nearly jumped on to her cheeks when she saw who was suddenly doing all the shouting!

'Rules? Rules?' roared Mr Olderfleet. 'I object. Don't talk to me about rules, Mister. *Look* at my children, they are shattered. I *object.*'

And he reached out to haul Knuckles in front of the organizing committee. Streams of tears ran down either side of Knuckles's nose like rivers that would never run dry, and the sight was truly shocking, for nobody had ever seen him cry.

One of the organizers tackled Mr Olderfleet.

'Don't make an exhibition of yourself, sir.'

'Exhibition!' repeated Mr Olderfleet. Saliva exploded from his lips. 'Let me tell you something, nothing beats the exhibition you've made of these children. What is the age limit for this competition?'

'Under twelve, of course.'

'I see. Under twelve.' Mr Olderfleet pointed at Maurice Baimes, who stood by as confused as anybody else. 'I happen to know this boy, and if he's eleven, you'll be eighteen again on your next birthday. Is he disqualified, too?' The official looked at his colleagues for help. 'Well? I object, I object, I object!'

Flute! thought Penny Brown. And in front of the town's mayor!

The organizers went into a huddle again, and talked among themselves for so long that some of the crowd began to drift off home.

Then one of them spoke up. He didn't sound happy.

'In view of certain . . . eh . . . irregularities . . . brought to our attention and after investigating the . . . eh . . . facts . . . our decision is that all results must stand. I call upon her Worship the Mayor to present the trophy to the captain of this year's winners—the All-Stars.'

'That's us!' piped up Shorty.

His brother couldn't move. Penny Brown had to set him in motion with a push. Knuckles wiped his wet face with a mucky sleeve as he stepped forward to receive the trophy. The crowd came alive with a great and satisfying roar, and Gowso's cousins threw themselves about like a troupe of chimpanzees escaped from the circus.

Mr. Olderfleet
Penny Brown
Mandy Taylor
Knuckles
Shorty
Legweak
Mavis Purvis
Gowso
Smudge
Caretakers dog
Jimmy Zest

# \* Jimmy Zest All-Stars \*

The Jimmy Zest All-Stars sat on the chippy wall discussing many things.

Mandy Taylor gave a boring description of a funicular railway in faraway Switzerland, and the others listened politely, purely because she'd saved that penalty. There were even plans afoot to buy her a replacement goldfish as a token of their undying appreciation.

Shorty passed the time by breathing on his winners' medal and shining it yet again on his chest. He had not taken it off since the tournament and intended to wear it in bed that night.

Jimmy Zest said, 'It's a fake, you know, that big chain round the mayor's neck. It's not real gold.'

'How do you know that, Zesty?'

'I asked her.'

Where on earth did people get the nerve to do such things, wondered Mandy Taylor.

Penny Brown changed the subject. 'Anyway, I've decided that I quite like him, now. He's very fair, you know.'

'Exactly who are we talking about?' asked Legweak.

'Mr Olderfleet. Did you see the way he stuck up for us? I thought he was going to eat those people alive. Well, he wouldn't do that unless he liked us, would he? I think we should admit we were wrong about him.'

There seemed to be general agreement about that remark, even from Knuckles, who was hoping to see Maurice Baimes walking by.